To Piper,

Be the s

!

Best wishes,

THE SHINING ADVENTURES OF
SHELPA McSTORM

The Shining Adventures of Shelpa McStorm

SCOTT SUSSMAN

ILLUSTRATIONS BY

NOEL TUAZON

A portion of proceeds from the sale of *The Shining Adventures of Shelpa McStorm* will be donated to First Book, a nonprofit organization that provides new books for children in need. Learn more about their work at www.firstbook.org.

Library of Congress Control Number: 2015904139
ISBN: 978-0-9829506-6-1
First printing 2016

Printed in the United States of America

Octopus Ink Press
9462 Swift Avenue
Fountain Valley, CA 92708

www.octopusinkpress.com

OCTOPUS INK
PRESS

FOR FRANCESCA

CHAPTER 1

HAD SHE STAYED on the beach like he told her to, like her parents insisted, none of this madness would have happened. The forest was forbidden, off limits, the one dangerous place on the planet, and what does she do? But the story is already ahead of itself. Let's go back to the beginning . . .

Birds flew above Sandy Beach, riding the wind on their wings as Shelpa McStorm rode the waves on a surfboard. He sped over the top of a rising wave and then dropped onto its face. The wave curled over his head, forming a tube that sucked him inside, where hundreds of fish the size of his fingers raced to keep up with him. Water sprayed all around him as he dipped forward and shot out of the tube. He cut back toward the wave, charged up its lip, and launched off the peak into the air. After flipping several somersaults, he landed with all ten

of his toes hanging over the front end of the board. One foot was too far forward, though, and he managed to hang ten for only an instant before he slipped sideways and splashed into the water.

Shelpa paddled to shore, removed the surfboard's leash from his ankle, and tucked the board under his arm. Walking along the water toward where his family had laid down their towels, he watched as a purple bird plunged into the ocean right in front of him. After resurfacing with a peanut butter and jelly fish twitching in its beak, the bird bolted back into the sky but dropped its meal, which flopped on the sand at Shelpa's feet. Shelpa picked up the peanut butter and jelly fish, cold and slimy in his hands, and tossed it into the air.

The bird swooped down and snatched its food. As the bird ascended, one of its feathers came free. Shelpa caught the falling feather, adjusted his grip on the surfboard, and tucked the feather behind his ear.

Waves washed up on the shore in front of Big Toe Hotel, leaving bubbling holes where sea spiders burrowed into the sand. Shelpa stopped to inspect the various shapes and colors of the seashells on the beach. He knelt next to a star-shaped red one and slid a finger over its textured exterior, not noticing the large wave racing toward him. Next thing he knew, he was tumbling head over heels. He rolled like a bowling ball until the wave receded, leaving him flat on his back with a mouthful of sand.

After sitting up, wiping his eyes, and coughing up half the beach, he saw Smiley Ray staring at him with her sapphire blue eyes. The hint of a smile betrayed her amusement. When she saw he was okay, she wagged her blossom head and lay back in her lounge chair, turning her red-petaled face toward the sky.

Shelpa's shining eyes glowed as he laughed and wiped sand off his arms and neck. He retrieved the surfboard and returned it to the rack of rentable equipment not far from where his mother sat. As soon as he reached her, he glanced at the table next to his towel. "Hey, Ma, my ice cream coming?"

Mrs. McStorm was covering herself with lotion. She set the bottle on her lap, and her radiant white hair slid to the side as she tilted her head. "The waiter said they're out of ice cream."

Shelpa's cheeks puffed, and the shine radiating from his body grew brighter. "You gotta be kidding me! How can they be out of ice cream?"

"Isn't it early for ice cream?" Smiley asked.

Shelpa's eyes widened incredulously. "It's *never* early for ice cream!"

"It's not the end of the universe," Mrs. McStorm said. "You can order something else—preferably something healthy like raisin oatmeal or spinach soup."

"Yuck!" Shelpa said, flicking sand grains off his towel. "Anyway, I don't see how you can just sit around here. Let's go build a sand castle or catch sea spiders or something."

"Or get clobbered by a wave." Smiley giggled between the tips of her leaves.

Shelpa looked at Smiley and wondered if she needed to be watered—and if so, how often. "Very funny. Had I seen that wave coming, I'd have surfed it to the tip of tomorrow."

"But you didn't," Smiley said, smirking, "and it knocked you to the trough of today."

CHAPTER 2

"THE TROUGH OF today," Shelpa repeated while he wrapped a towel around his waist and slipped out of his wetsuit. "That was so funny I forgot to laugh." He grabbed his blue-gray overalls from under the table, put them on, and tightened both straps. Then he plucked the purple feather from behind his ear and slipped it into one of his hip pockets.

Hearing voices, Shelpa turned to see his father approaching. He was as luminous as a lightbulb and was glowing so intensely his lightning-white skin sparkled right through his T-shirt and jeans. He was reading from a ring-bound booklet, with Smiley's father—a tall, lanky rose—at his side, lumbering along on his roots. Though Mr. Ray was a hand taller, Shelpa's father's shine made them appear the same height.

Mr. McStorm licked his twinkling thumb and flipped the page. His hair puffed out like white smoke as he read aloud: "'The Xyzyx—half sun, half moon—is a rare star composed of gases and other materials that magnetically channel into its hollow core the thoughts, memories, dreams, and fantasies of every mind in its vicinity. As clouds crossing the sky are sculpted by the wind, condense, and make rain, these transformed thoughts and experiences return to Panacea as fantastic events, incredible creatures, and never-before-imagined flora and fauna.'"

Mrs. McStorm cut in. "What did you find out at the reception desk?"

Mr. McStorm looked up and smiled, revealing glowing white teeth and shimmering eyes. "There's an orientation in ten minutes. We don't have to attend, but it's highly recommended."

"What's it about?" asked Mrs. McStorm.

"The details about staying safe and stuff. But I don't see why we need to go. We've got this guidebook that explains pretty much everything. Basically, just stay on the beach."

Mrs. Ray was plucking wilted petals from her blossom. "Hear that, kids? Nobody leaves the beach."

"Yes, Mama," Smiley said.

"Does going in the water count as leaving the beach?" Shelpa asked.

"I don't think so," Mr. McStorm said, setting the

booklet on the table. "You can go in the water if you want."

Just then, a gorilla leaped up from the sea with arms and legs outstretched. The ape sailed through the air and then belly flopped on the water with a great splash. A dozen or so other guests on the beach whistled, applauded, and cheered.

"Did you see that?" Mr. Ray asked, his voice squeaking like a loose wagon wheel. He clapped his leaves. "This is going to be great! You never know what to expect here— all kinds of fun stuff. Like the guidebook says, everyone's experience is different and never the same twice."

A knife approached them, hopping on its handle and wearing a black-and-white tuxedo. Bowing, the knife said, "Welcome to Panacea. I'll be your host for this morning's orientation. The meeting starts soon, so please head on over to the lounge. We'll walk together from there to the assembly room."

Shelpa moaned. "Do we have to?"

"Actually," the knife said to the parents, "the kids can stay here if they like. If they need anything, there's a lifeguard on duty at all times." The knife bent forward, pointing the tip of its blade at the lifeguard station.

Glancing over his shoulder toward the center of the beach, Shelpa saw a lifeguard tower with marine-green panels and banana-yellow railing. A white ladder rested against the side, and a huddled form slumped on the platform, which was also accessible by a ramp.

"Fine, then," Mr. Ray said. "We're on our way. Thanks!"

The knife nodded and hopped away.

Mr. McStorm squared his shoulders and said, "Okay, kids. We'll be back as soon as possible. I don't imagine orientation could last too long. Until then, Shelpa, you're in charge."

Shelpa's jaw dropped, and his eyes shot open. Beads of sweat formed on his brow. His muscles seemed to deflate inside his overalls. He looked at his mother and saw her staring at his father. He also caught Smiley's parents exchanging a glance.

"Got that, son?"

Shelpa gulped, and his fingers and toes tingled. "Yeah, Dad. Okay."

"If you kids need anything," Mr. McStorm said, "get what you want, and charge it to the room."

"And, Smiley," Mrs. Ray said, "remember to water yourself. She indicated a silver container with a curved spout that sat on the sand by Smiley's chair. "You don't want to wilt like last time."

"Don't worry, Mama. I'll be fine. After all, what could go wrong?"

CHAPTER 3

AS THEIR PARENTS walked away, Shelpa saw his mother lean into his father. She was whispering, but he heard her say, "Are you sure about this?"

"It's about time," Mr. McStorm said. "He deserves…"

Shelpa missed the rest, and soon the lounge doors slid shut behind his parents as they entered the hotel.

Smiley scooped up some sand and eyed Shelpa while sifting grains between her leaves. In a sweet, melodic voice, she asked, "Having fun yet?"

Shelpa scratched his nose and sniffed. "I wouldn't mind some ice cream." He looked over at Big Toe Hotel, a white-and-silver building shaped like a huge foot, with the reception area and most of the patio located in the big toe. He could see the forest on either side of the hotel, and far beyond the hotel, deep in the forest, rose a brown mountain, its highest peak obscured by clouds.

"I know we just met an hour ago, so pardon my manners, but it's a funny thing, the way you shine like that."

"On Shine, where I'm from, everybody does."

"Why?"

Shelpa stretched out on his towel, hands behind his head. "For one thing, shining regulates our body temperatures."

"How hot can you get? Hot enough to boil water with your hands?"

"No. Shining doesn't work like that."

"What happens if you shine too brightly? Can you burn up?"

"Of course not." Shelpa stared up at the sky. "At least I don't think I can."

"So how does it work?"

"It's a chemical reaction that happens in our skin.

Something to do with enzymes and oxygen. I'm not really sure."

"Can you control how brightly you shine?"

"Sort of. Sometimes. It depends. Like when I'm anxious or excited, I shine more, and when I'm tired or depressed, I shine less."

Smiley grabbed her watering can. She tilted the nozzle above her blossom, sprinkling water on her petals and leaves. Smiley was from Pix, a garden paradise inhabited by flowers. "How long have you surfed?"

"Since before I can remember. My mom says I was born surfing."

"Looks like fun."

"Have you ever tried?"

"Nope."

Shelpa turned onto his side and propped himself up on an elbow. "Well, it's definitely fun, but it takes time to learn."

"Oh, I think I could do it."

Shelpa sat up and twisted all the way around. He watched Smiley set the watering can on the sand. Beaded with hundreds of glistening drops of water, she looked at him and winked. Shelpa shook his head. "I'll tell you what. Feel free to tackle those waves whenever you like. You'll see what I mean. Afterward, if you need a tip or two, I'd be happy to help."

Shelpa grabbed the guidebook from the table and flipped to the first page. After skimming through several sentences, he read the next one out loud: "'Please report any injuries to the first-aid station located in the hotel's pinky toe.'" Speaking over his shoulder to Smiley, he said, "They ought to call it the *stinky* toe, considering you have to go there for injuries. Let's hope we never see the inside of that place, right?"

Smiley shrugged her stem and then rested her blossom on a leaf. "Obviously."

Shelpa read on: "'Open fires are permitted but must comply with the guidelines listed under Park Parameters.'" He turned toward Smiley. "You know what we say on my planet? It takes one tree to make a million matchsticks, but one matchstick to burn down the whole forest. Interesting, eh?"

Smiley yawned, and her whole body sagged as she slouched in her chair. "Yes, Shelpa, interesting."

"Listen to this: 'All sockets are solar-power compatible.' Wow, how many sockets in the universe *aren't* solar-power compatible? I'd imagine that's a given nowadays." At the bottom of the page, Shelpa noticed the word WARNING printed in all capitals and highlighted in red. Again, he read out loud: "'Never leave the group during forest excursions. If by chance you become separated, do not wait to be found. Find your way out of the forest immediately. Guests stranded in the forest after nightfall will be trapped forever. They will forget who and where they are, and they will wander in circles for the rest of their lives, with no chance of escape or being rescued.'"

Shelpa slapped the guidebook shut and set it on the table. "Wow! What do you think of that, Smiley?"

There was no response.

"Smiley . . . ?"

He spun around. Smiley's chair was empty.

Shelpa jumped to his feet and scanned the beach area, then all around Big Toe Hotel. Not seeing her, he was about to scream for help, but then he spotted her in the ocean. She was gliding on a surfboard along the face of a wave. Shelpa was sure she would wipe out, and he grinned as the wave broke over her. He took a step toward the lifeguard tower, laughing to himself and expecting to see her topple, blossom over roots. But then Smiley sailed out of the tube, just as he had done earlier. Blinking repeatedly, he watched as she angled up the wave's face, dropped onto its shoulder, and cut back into the breaking mix of bubbles and froth.

Then Smiley did something Shelpa had never seen before. She pitched around to the right, slipped past the breaking wave she had been riding, and reentered the tube from behind. Once again she shot out of the barrel's mouth, and this time she launched into the air with her stem flat against the board and her leaves gripping the rails as she spun in circles. After splashing back on the water, she popped up onto her roots, bent forward, balanced her blossom on the board, and lifted her roots in the air. Pushing up on her leaves, she moved into a handstand position and rode into shore, skidding into the wet sand.

Shelpa's jaw had fallen open so wide he could have caught a fish in his mouth. After Smiley had dragged the surfboard back to the rack, she sat down in her lounge chair behind his towel.

Shelpa wiped his forehead with the back of his hand. Light-headed and short of breath, he managed to utter one word. "How?"

CHAPTER 4

SMILEY GRABBED THE watering can and started rinsing the salt water off her roots. "Watching you, I understood you've got to synchronize with the wave, with the ocean—with all of nature. Well, I'm a flower. I *am* nature. You are, too, actually, but your vibrations aren't harmonized. That's why you slipped and fell."

Shelpa massaged his stomach, trying to calm the butterflies in his belly. Smiley's expertise with the surf-board had made him feel queasy. "What do you mean, my vibrations aren't harmonized?"

"I mean you have to be in sync with yourself to be at peace with everything around you. If you reject any part of yourself—an emotion, a memory—you won't be in harmony, and that can affect other areas of your life. When you're not in harmony, you're off balance, like a song that's out of tune."

Shelpa scratched the back of his neck. "I don't understand."

"Think of it this way. A damaged key will have trouble opening a lock, and it might not work at all. Harmonized vibrations are like a perfectly shaped key. When you're harmonized, instead of scraping against nature, you flow along with it. Being in harmony can unlock doors you didn't even know were there, which explains how I was able to surf so well without any experience."

As Shelpa pondered Smiley's words, he heard a wave rush up the sand and felt the white water bubbling against the bottoms of his feet. He looked at the crescent-shaped beach in front of him and then at the forest. As he gazed at the trees, an eerie sensation raised the hairs on the back of his neck. Several trees were waving, beckoning him with their branches. "Leave the beach," he heard them saying. "The forest can help you." Shelpa rubbed his eyes and blinked. When he looked again, he saw normal trees swaying in the breeze.

His eyebrows arched. "Did you just—"

"Let's take a walk," Smiley interrupted.

Shelpa waved his hand through the air as if erasing words written there. "Not a chance. Stay here where I can keep an eye on you."

"I don't understand why your dad put you in charge. You're not much older than I am."

"Sure about that? How old are you?"

Smiley sat up straight. "Thirty-six."

"Thirty-six? You're not thirty-six! Thirty-six what? Weeks?"

"Thirty-six seasons."

"Oh, okay, *seasons*. That I understand. By Shine standards, I'm three years, or twelve *seasons*, older than you. That's probably why I'm in charge."

Smiley rubbed the side of her blossom against her chair, causing a petal to come loose. "Ouch!"

Shelpa pointed at the detached petal tumbling in the breeze. "What's up with that?"

"Nothing. It's normal."

"And it hurts?"

"Just a little, like a pinch."

"Don't you worry about that?"

"Course not. They grow back, and it sort of tickles when they do."

Shelpa's shine increased. "Cool."

"Anyway, I meant both of us taking a walk. Together." Smiley reached forward and grabbed the guidebook. She flipped through the pages.

Shelpa turned toward her. "Wait until our parents get back, please."

"Look at this." Smiley pointed at a paragraph. "The guidebook says, 'The heat, haze, and illusory properties of the Xyzyx light can play tricks on your senses. For this reason, guests are warned to question what they see, smell, and hear, as certain events may be unreal. This phenomenon is one of Panacea's main attractions, but also one of its primary dangers. What appears to be a solid trail could turn out to be a perilous cliff, or a seemingly harmless boulder could be a huge, constricting snake. If you would like to venture into the forest or other areas, excursions led by our expert survival guides can be booked at Big Toe Hotel's reception desk.' Awesome! Let's go check out the forest."

"Are you kidding? Didn't you just hear what you read? We need a survival guide for that."

Smiley fixed Shelpa with her piercing blue eyes. "It can't hurt to peek between the trees, right? Let's just look."

"Not right now. When your parents return, you can go wherever you want." Shelpa turned again to face the sea. He could see several birds playing hide-and-seek inside a cloud. Most of the birds were clearly visible to Shelpa—a purple wing here, a blue tail there—and he chuckled as the searching red bird struggled to find its friends.

"Come on," Smiley said. "Where's your sense of adventure?"

"It's out there in the water, which counts as the beach. *Not* in the forest."

"Okay," Smiley said. "If you don't want to go, fine. Nobody's forcing you."

Shelpa raised his voice. "Sorry, but I have my reasons. If we had a pair of binoculars, you could look into the forest from here. If you want, I'll go ask the lifeguard if there are some we can use. If not, maybe we can rent them at the reception desk. How's that for a fair compromise?"

Glancing toward the forest, Shelpa thought he saw a scoop of vanilla ice cream floating above the trees. Shielding his eyes from the Xyzyx light, he realized he was looking at a distant cloud drifting over the treetops. He nibbled the edge of his thumb and lay on his back again. Answering his own question, he said, "I'd say it's more than fair. Of course, if nobody has binoculars, we'll just have to wait until *after* our parents get back."

A gust of wind sent sand grains flecking his neck and shoulder. Sitting up and turning toward Smiley, he saw her chair was empty.

Shelpa again jumped to his feet, muscles flexed and nerves in a knot as he scanned the ocean and beach for her.

CHAPTER 5

SHELPA'S HEART HAMMERED. He took rasping breaths. Then he saw her, the size of a pea, striding toward a sign that stood where the forest met the beach. He started after her but stopped. Remembering the knife's words, he turned and marched toward the lifeguard station. "Obviously, she won't listen to me," he said to himself, "but maybe she'll listen to the lifeguard."

He discovered that the lifeguard was a wrinkled old walrus with gray-brown skin pocked with scars and spotted with blemishes. Sprawled on its back with its massive belly bulging in the air and fins dangling to the sides, it was snoring like a chainsaw slicing through a tree trunk. The walrus's tusks were chipped and chewed, its whiskers frayed. Its lifeguard shirt seemed about to burst at the seams.

Fish heads and clamshells littered the platform.

Cringing at the stink, Shelpa stepped forward. "Excuse me. You see that flower over there by the sign? Her parents said she's not supposed to go over there and that I—"

The walrus interrupted him with a snore like nuts and bolts rattling in a toolbox. Spittle bubbled between its flabby lips, and its whiskers went straight as pencils.

Shelpa poked a luminous finger into the walrus's belly, hoping to wake it up, but his finger sunk into the creature's blubber as if he had reached into a bowl of jelly. Shelpa glanced over his shoulder at Smiley. She was gazing up at the sign now. He could see her blossom face moving from side to side as she read its words.

Turning back to the walrus, he removed his hand and shouted, "Lifeguard, please, I need your help." Shelpa pinched the lifeguard's fin. The walrus chuckled in its sleep and then rolled onto its side, presenting its enormous backside to Shelpa's face.

Shelpa gave up, surveyed the area around Big Toe Hotel, and noticed that all the silverware—forks, knives, spoons—were gone.

Probably participating in the orientation, he thought.

He turned to the only other guests still on the beach. The first was a huge gargoyle crouched over its bony legs and clutching its knees to its chest. Half man, half monkey, with shriveled skin and hooks at the ends of its arms, the grotesque creature stared at the sea with a stony expression. As an insect flew near its face, the gargoyle's tongue shot out and slurped the bug into its fanged mouth.

The second guest was a red-scaled dragon as big as a fire engine. It had smoking nostrils and razor-sharp spikes lining its spine. The monstrous beast held a bottle of lotion in one front paw and was slathering lotion onto one of its webbed wings with the other front paw.

Best not to get either of them involved, Shelpa thought.

He considered heading over to the hotel and asking for help at the reception desk, if anybody was there, but then he saw Smiley moving toward the trees. "She wouldn't," he said to himself, watching with wide-open eyes.

Just then, she pulled aside a curtain of dangling vines and disappeared into the forest.

"Oh boy!" Shelpa said, his shine sparkling intensely. He smacked the lifeguard's flipper and screamed, "You fat lard! Get up off your blubber!"

Still snoring, the walrus exhaled with the sputtering gargle an old engine makes when struggling to start.

Shelpa turned and ran. "Smiley! Get back here!"

CHAPTER 6

SHELPA TRIPPED AND stumbled over the soft sand, his heart bouncing around like a stone in his chest. "Not again!" he said to himself. "NOT AGAIN!" The more ground he covered, the more distant the trees seemed.

Shining like the midday sun, he finally reached the sign. As he fought to catch his breath, he read: DANGER! DUE TO UNPREDICTABLE CIRCUMSTANCES CAUSED BY THE XYZYX, WE REQUEST THAT YOU REMAIN ON THE BEACH AT ALL TIMES. KINDEST REGARDS, THE MANAGEMENT

Shelpa whistled through his teeth. "Boy oh boy, this can't be happening!" He brushed back a strand of his silvery hair and charged into the forest. He scrambled over toppled trees and wove between thorny bushes, passing other signs: STOP! GO BACK! ENTER AT YOUR OWN RISK! YOU'D HAVE TO BE CRAZY TO CONTINUE!

The air was cooler in the shade of the forest, but Shelpa's quick pace warmed him as he squished over soggy patches of crushed leaves and splintered sticks. Slivers of light penetrated the web of limbs and leaves overhead. Humming insects and strange quacks and oinks echoed all around. He smelled wet wood and rotting vegetation.

Shelpa glowed steadily. He worried about falling off a cliff or being attacked by a boulder as he passed. Though he had never practiced any martial arts, he brought his hands up in a karate chop stance, ready to defend himself. Then he moved forward cautiously, glancing above and behind, occasionally slicing the air with a spontaneous chop, and jumping at every strange sound from the surrounding trees.

After several minutes and half a dozen karate chops, he started to relax and search for signs of Smiley—root prints, a petal—while calling her name. "Smiley! *Smiley!*"

In a clearing, he found what he was looking for: a red petal lodged between two stones. This was a sure sign that Smiley had been there, but two trails led in different directions. The first zigzagged off between white trees as curled as corkscrews. The second curved away into a dark grove where swarms of wasps hovered around several hives, and a green, poisonous-looking mist clouded the air. "No chance of Smiley going in there," he said to himself. "Boy oh boy. I hope nothing happens to her—or to *me*." He took a deep breath and headed toward the trail leading through the white trees.

CHAPTER 7

SHELPA HIKED OVER the zigzagging trail, running his hands through his hair and scouring the ground for fresh signs of Smiley. White moss covered the trees, clumping at the tops to resemble giant cotton balls. The trail was white, too, blanketed with dust. Kicked up by Shelpa's feet, the dust rose in clouds and powdered the bushes. The air was lighter here and smelled like peppermint.

The tall stalks of snow-white grass glistened with dew, and when Shelpa plucked a sticklike branch from a nearby tree, water soaked him from head to toe. Dripping wet and gritting his teeth, he tramped along the path, stripping the stick of its leaves. Bushes with fluffy white flowers like dandelion seed heads grew thigh-high on both sides of the trail. Shelpa gripped the stick until his knuckles whitened, and then aimed a cutting sweep at the flower on his right. The flower exploded in a cloud of petals and white fluff.

Impressed with the results, Shelpa continued along, swinging the stick back and forth. "Where in the universe is she?" He aimed the stick at another flower and slashed sideways. *Kaboom!* Another blast fogged the air.

"I'm going to squeeze the red out of her petals when I find her." He stopped and looked around. Then he shivered and added, "*If* I find her."

He attacked more flowers, punishing any plant that chanced to grow too near the path.

Slash!

"I can't believe this is happening!"

Thwack!

"Why me?"

Swish!

"This vacation is turning into a nightmare!"

Fwap!

As he walked through the haze of petals and fluff, Shelpa's throat started to sting. He felt he was choking, invisible hands strangling him. He snapped the stick in half and hurled one half at the bushes and the other against a wall of corkscrew trees. His ears pounded as blood flooded his head.

He rushed forward out of the mist until he could breathe more normally. His jaw ached from grinding his teeth, and his hands had cramped from clenching his fists. "Getting angry's no good," he said to himself. "I've got to relax. Think strai—"

Just then, a sharp pain stabbed into his heel. "Arghhhhhhhhh!" he howled, and jumped around on one leg while holding the injured foot with his hands.

A voice as quiet as a whisper said, "Got him!" and then, booming, screamed, "HIDE, STAPLES, HIDE! THE STAPLER IS HERE! THE STAPLER IS HERE!"

Bushes rustled, branches swayed, and tiny voices screamed, "The stapler! Run!"

Looking down, Shelpa saw a little tack glaring up at him. Holding a megaphone at its side, the tack said,

"Shame on you! What kind of scoundrel terrorizes helpless staples?"

"What?" Shelpa asked, cupping a hand to his ear and crouching. "I'm sorry. I can't hear you."

"Don't play stupid with me, stapler. I know what you're up to." The tack turned to the surrounding forest. Holding the megaphone to its mouth, it shouted, "STAY WHERE YOU ARE, STAPLES! DON'T BE TRICKED! REMEMBER WHAT HAPPENED LAST TIME!"

With the tack's words amplified through the megaphone, its voice was deafening. Shelpa covered his ears.

The tack stared up at him. "Don't try any tricks on me. I'll poke your eyes out before you can say 'bulletin board.' Now get out of here!"

Shelpa placed a hand on his chest. "I'm not a stapler. I don't even know what you're talking about. I was just passing through when you stuck me in the foot."

"If you try to pass through here, partner, you'll get more than a prick in the foot! Now hear this: These staples are under my protection. If you try any funny business, I will stick you where it hurts the most!" The tack kicked up a small cloud of dust.

"I promise not to harm the staples. I don't even know where they are. Just let me pass, please."

"What do you take me for, a fool? If you think I'm going to let you at them, then you are *one stupid stapler!*"

"Fine. Tell me one thing, and I'll go. I'm looking for a friend. She's a red flower. I've got to get her back to the beach. Have you seen her?"

"What do you take me for, a fool? Why would a flower want to go to the beach? The beach is dry sand and salt water. Flowers need wet soil and *fresh* water! Stapler, your presence here is intrusive and undesirable. I'm not going to warn you again. Leave!"

"I'm not a stapler! Why do you think I am?"

"Why do I think . . . ?" The tack paced back and forth before Shelpa's feet. "I'll tell you what. I'm willing to make a deal. You turn around and go away, and I'll let you live."

Shelpa's heart was racing. He breathed in and out several times, then turned around and started walking away. "Fine. If I can't pass, I'll go back to the beach."

The tack followed him a few steps, hopping along until convinced Shelpa was sincere. When Shelpa glanced over his shoulder and saw the tack returning to its post, he whirled around and ran back. He heard bushes shudder and leaves shake as the hiding staples panicked, alerting the tack. The tack turned to strike, but Shelpa leaped into the air, sailed over the tack, and landed safely. He sprinted a good way down the trail before stopping to look back. Breathing heavily, he saw that the tack was nowhere in sight.

Hunched over with his hands on his knees, Shelpa shook his head. Smiley was gone. And what if he never found her? At least half an hour had passed since they had left the beach. Their parents were surely back by now and, finding neither him nor Smiley, were probably going bonkers. Should he turn around, let them know he was okay? He cringed at the idea of facing the tack again.

The tack would stick me, for sure, he thought. *And who knows where? Even if I got past the tack, what would I tell my parents, and hers? That Smiley was lost in the woods, and I abandoned her? No, I have to find her at any cost.*

Just then, he heard a chortling sound above him. Looking up, he saw a stork carrying a bundle in its beak. The stork flapped lower, steering toward Shelpa, and dropped the bundle. A parachute mushroomed open as the bundle drifted down, and then two feet appeared. As it landed, Shelpa saw that it was a blue-furred baby kangaroo.

The kangaroo hopped around him, gathering leaves in its paws and laying the leaves one by one on the trail by Shelpa's feet to spell out the word CLEVER. Seeing the word sent a jolt of electricity through his veins. Did the kangaroo mean the way he had outsmarted the tack? As Shelpa grinned, the kangaroo poked his shin with the tip of its tail, then aimed its tail upward. Shelpa glanced into the canopy of branches, twigs, and leaves above his head.

CHAPTER 7

He rubbed his chin and narrowed his eyes, and when he looked at the ground again, the kangaroo was gone.

CHAPTER 8

SWINGING HIS ARMS, Shelpa continued down the path. His feet sank in and then bounced back as though he were walking on a sponge. The air felt warmer and smelled of cinnamon. He saw an occasional petal and what seemed to be root prints, but he could not be sure they were Smiley's.

Soon he heard someone singing in a whining, throaty voice. The sound grew louder until, after rounding a bend, he saw a sombrero standing at the side of the path, sticking out its thumb.

"Hey, buddy, got room for a hitchhiker? I don't bother nobody. Juzt zit on your head and keep quiet. I don't mean to zay I ignore you or nothing, juzt that I can be a bit of a chatterbox."

Shelpa hesitated. He was in a hurry. But then again, maybe the hat could help. After all, four eyes were better than two. Nodding, he said, "Okay, sure."

The sombrero slapped itself on the brim and said, "Fantaztic!"

Shelpa picked up the hat and placed it on his head. Its brim covered his eyes, so the sombrero tipped back and forth like a ringing bell, tightening itself to fit. Finally comfortable, the hat leaned forward and examined him. "You zeem to be a nize fellow. By the way, where you headed?"

"I'm looking for someone," Shelpa said, continuing down the trail. "Have you seen a red flower?"

"A red one? All I know iz the lazt time I waz looking for a flower, I ended up in the middle of No Man'z Land. There waz thiz two-headed giant zleeping in a cave, and az I entered, zuddenly the headz woke up. I tried to run, but one of itz handz caught me before I could ezcape. The handz tugged me back and forth, fighting for who would wear me. Az they zcreamed and zpit, one zaid it found me firzt while the other shouted, 'Zo what! I zaw him zecond, and two iz bigger than one!'"

As the hat rambled on, Shelpa only half listened, concentrating on where he was going. In time, he started to feel tired, and the hat began to weigh on his head. He noticed a bush with sparkling leaves and remembered having passed one like it.

"Haven't we been through here already?"

"Here? No zir!"

"Are you sure? I've seen that bush."

"That bush iz one of hundredz! Keep your eyez open. You'll zee many more."

Shelpa's mouth scrunched to the side. He considered ditching the hat but decided to wait. "Please let me know if you see any red flowers, or red petals even."

"Will do! But let me finish my ztory about the two-headed giant. Finally, while the headz were fighting about how many fingerz it takez to make a fizt, I fell to the floor and znuck away. Ever zince, I alwayz refuze to ride with anybody who haz more than one head. That'z why when I zaw you, I zaid to myzelf, 'Now here comez zomebody that lookz like a good kid, and only one head.'"

Shelpa's legs felt rubbery. He was breathing harder than he should have been. The hat continued to blab, as if any thought that came into its mind was worth sharing.

After a while, Shelpa noticed the bush with sparkling leaves again. This time, he also noticed a clump of rust-colored weeds he had seen before. When he recognized a heart-shaped rock he was about to step over, he said, "I'm sure something's wrong. We've passed this place twice already."

The sombrero said nothing.

"Did you hear me? I said we've passed this place already. Two times at least."

"You think zo?"

Shelpa stopped in his tracks, feeling weaker than ever. "Yes, I'm sure of it."

"Well, uh, where'd you zay you waz going?"

"I didn't. I said I was looking for a friend, and you're supposed to be helping."

"I'm on the lookout! You can count on me."

"But we're going in circles."

"Zo? What'z wrong with circlez?"

Shelpa yanked the hat off his head. Holding it firmly, he jabbed a finger into its brim. "Hey! What's going on here?"

The hat struggled to free itself from Shelpa's viselike grip. "Circlez are zafe. They lead you back to the zame place every time, zo you never get lozt."

"I knew it! Where are we?"

"Right back where we began. Zee the trunk of that tree?" The sombrero pointed with its thumb. "I carved my initialz into it while I waz waiting for a ride."

"Now what?" Shelpa set down the hat, which by now weighed as much as a pile of bricks, and trudged over to the tree to finger the grooves. "Maybe I should go back."

"You can't go back. Not more than a few ztepz anyway. Forward'z the only way through the forezt. Haven't you noticed?"

"But if we keep going in circles, we'll never get anywhere!"

"Exactly, going iz the important thing, not the getting there."

"What if I squeeze through those trees and head into the forest?"

"You can do that, I zuppoze. But heed my advize: You don't want to go in there. Truzt me, ztick to the trail. Come on. Let'z go. I'll tell you a ztory about a beard I met that made friendz by cracking jokez."

"Not a chance," Shelpa said. "You're wasting my time."

"Nothing of the kind. I'm juzt trying to help."

"If you want to help, wish me luck."

The sombrero stared at Shelpa while wagging its brim. "Luck? You're going to need more than that."

Shelpa squeezed through the trees that formed the forest's wall. The white moss, at first silky against his skin, grew coarse edges, and limbs reached out with sticklike fingers, catching the straps and pockets of his overalls. Branches and jutting roots crossed at various heights and angles, forcing him to fight to move forward a few inches. Brambles scratched his arms, and barbed-leaf bushes blocked his progress. Twigs snapped, branches broke, thorns scraped his neck and shoulders, and a stick ripped a pocket off the side of his overalls. When he ducked beneath the limbs of a splintered tree, a jagged branch gashed his shoulder. He winced at the pain.

Shelpa stopped to catch his breath. Surrounded by corkscrew trees and twisted nettles, he could see only inches in front of his face. Too committed to turn back, he continued forward. Weeds wrapped around his ankles, and creepers seized his calves. He yanked the weeds from the ground and tore out the creepers by their roots, pressing one foot forward at a time and occasionally reaching out a hand to grip a branch and pull himself along. Sweat coursed down his face as he battled for every step.

He heard cracking sticks and crunching leaves beyond some shrubs about five feet ahead of him. As he pushed forward he heard twigs snap, and saw a blue blur dash between bushes. He crawled around a tree, and there he saw sticks on the ground arranged to form the word DETERMINED. Shelpa sparkled with pleasure. The kangaroo? Was that what that blue blur had been? He shrugged his shoulders and, after one more push, broke through the wall of vegetation.

CHAPTER 9

THOUGH SHELPA'S ELBOWS were skinned and the gash on his shoulder smarted, the dark landscape he saw made him forget his pain. Blood-black clouds smothered the sky, casting shadows and gloom on the splintered trees below. The air felt cold and clammy and reeked of rot and decay. While floundering over brittle chunks of what he thought were dirt clods and sticks, Shelpa tripped on a rock and landed face-first on the ground. Raising his head, he found himself staring into the eye sockets of a skull. His heart froze, and his throat constricted at the skull's cold, unblinking stare.

The skull's jawbone jerked up and down, and Shelpa heard its scratchy voice say, "Beware!"

Shelpa lurched upright and jumped back, horrified. His left foot broke through a ribcage as he landed.

Several ribs cracked, but the jagged edges of the others trapped his leg. Trying to keep his teeth from chattering, he asked, "W-w-what did you s-s-say?"

The skull, resting on top of a heap of bones, stared up at Shelpa. "Why are you here? Where are you going?"

Shivers crept up Shelpa's spine as he struggled to pull his leg free. He opened his mouth to speak, but nothing, not even air, came out.

"Listen to me! If you continue that way, you'll end up like me, a bonehead."

Shelpa saw only lifeless trees, their branches dripping with slime. "What's down there?" Shelpa managed to mumble.

"Nothing but bones, brother, nothing but bones. Heed my advice. Turn back while you've still got a life to lose."

"Why do you say that?"

"Because I've suffered longer than you've been alive. Believe me, this place is poison. Evil is everywhere!"

"Well, I can't go back now. It's impossible. And besides, I'm looking for someone."

The skull howled. "Futile! Useless! A waste of time! Nothing can bring her back."

Just then, something clutched Shelpa's right ankle, cutting off his circulation. He saw a skeleton hand wrinkling his pant leg. Hearing scraping sounds, he stared across the field of bones at dozens of other hands crawling toward him. He lifted his leg and kicked violently, but the hand held on.

"See what I'm saying? Why fight? You'll never leave here alive."

Shelpa panicked. He wrenched his leg out of the ribcage, snapping three more ribs, and staggered on, dragging the skeleton hand. He tripped and fell, blinded by terror, then got back to his feet and stumbled forward. No matter how far he advanced, he could still hear the skull's voice in his ear, warning, "Beware!"

More hands converged, crawling out from between bones and appearing from holes in the ground. A fierce wind wailed in his ears and blinded him with bone dust. Confused and disoriented, Shelpa continued to stumble over bones while slapping at the hand clinging to his ankle. He refused to surrender. He kept falling but regained his feet again and again. Finally, a skull with a fractured cranium glared up at him.

"Fine," the cracked skull said, "go wherever you want. We can't fight your fate."

At that, the wind eased, and releasing his ankle, the skeleton hand fell to the ground and shattered. Shelpa dropped to his knees, spitting out dust. After wiping his eyes, he stood and emptied the bone dust from his pockets. While he tightened the straps of his overalls, he saw something drop from the sky. He squinted, trying to see through the shadows as he walked forward. He heard crunching, followed by footsteps bounding away. Coming to a grassy clearing, he looked down and saw a word composed of bones: COURAGEOUS. The sight raised goose bumps on his arms and sent a shudder of excitement up his spine.

Still, he wondered, *what do these words mean?*

CHAPTER 10

AFTER LEAVING THE boneyard through a rusty gate, Shelpa hiked up a pebbled slope fringed by patches of grass and weeds. The path ended at a bluff overlooking a massive black-and-white chessboard with an ivory-colored castle in the farthest right corner. He saw knights and bishops, along with several pawns, but no kings or queens. A gentle wind had scattered the clouds, allowing the Xyzyx to shine down in columns of light. For the first time since entering the forest, he could see the Xyzyx itself—its face was clenched tight as a fist, as if suffering a splitting headache. It had red-rimmed eyes with dark circles underneath and a runny nose. Soon it began sniffling, sneezing, and coughing as if fighting off an infection. Shelpa was reminded of his own face when he was sick with the flu.

Looking for Smiley, Shelpa spotted a trail that snaked down from where he was standing to the first row of

squares. He was halfway down when he heard a scream
for help. He saw that someone had fallen inside one of
the black squares and was hanging on with one hand.

"I'm coming!" Shelpa yelled, sprinting to the rescue. When he reached the square, he grabbed the hand,
hoisting it onto a bordering white square.

Shelpa's mouth fell open. He had saved an arm with
a hand for a head.

The hand had two eyes and a toothless mouth stretching across its palm. Balancing on the ball of its elbow, the
arm fidgeted its thumb to keep balanced. "Thank you,
thank you, thank you!" The arm shook Shelpa's hand
with its head and then tipped back and forth as its thumb
jerked awkwardly. "Do you have any idea how long I've
been holding on?"

"No, how long?"

"Forever!"

Shelpa leaned over the square, whose sides were as long as lampposts, and stared down. "What's down there?"

The head grabbed him with its fingers and yanked him back. "Are you crazy? You don't want that to be *your* square, do you?"

"What do you mean, *my* square?"

The arm's eyes blinked repeatedly, and its mouth frowned. "Listen, chap, if you fall down there, that's it. You disappear."

"Why? Where does it go?"

"That's just it. Nobody knows where it goes. No one who has ever fallen in has returned to tell us."

Shelpa chewed on the inside of his cheek.

"You're not from around these parts, are you?" the arm asked. "What are you doing here?"

"I'm looking for a friend. She's a flower."

"Well, if she's fallen into any of these black squares, you're never going to see her again."

Shelpa's voice cracked as he asked, "What if she *has* fallen down a square? How would I know?"

The arm's hand bent back at the wrist, and its breath blasted Shelpa's face as it spoke. "You wouldn't! But the king might."

"Which king? Where? You mean in that castle?"

But before the arm could answer, another voice shouted, "Help! Somebody, please!" Several squares away, a second arm was hanging by its head.

With no time to lose, Shelpa jumped from white square to white square, rushing to save the second arm.

After he had pulled it out onto a white square, the rescued arm poised on the tip of its elbow and shook Shelpa's hand. "Thank you, thank you, thank you. Do you realize how long I've been hanging here?"

"Forever?"

"And a day!" The arm rocked back and forth.

Shelpa pointed to the castle. "Do you happen to know anything about the king who lives in that ca—?"

He was interrupted by another arm screaming, "Help, please, somebody!"

Scanning the chessboard, Shelpa noticed arms fallen into black squares everywhere.

If I try to rescue every arm, he thought, *I'll never get out of the forest before nighttime.*

From above, he heard the stork's chortle, and he glanced up to see the kangaroo riding on its back. The clouds took on new shapes in the wake of the stork's wings, spelling out RATIONAL. Shelpa grinned. He was radiant. Then, avoiding the black squares and their mysterious darkness, he went from one white square to another, hurrying toward the castle.

CHAPTER 11

SHELPA FOUND THE castle's drawbridge up and the moat filled with inky water that smelled like sewage. He held his nose and circled the castle cautiously, looking for another way across. Finding none, he considered swimming across the moat, but he could see the long, meaty tentacles of some octopus-like creature floating on the water's surface. Then he noticed a black box with white polka dots sitting near the moat's edge. Shelpa approached the box and stooped down to reach the Z-shaped handle sticking out from its side. A circus-like song played as he wound the handle. When the music built to a climax, he heard a click—and, at the same instant, noticed a shadow behind him. As he whipped around to face whoever it was, the someone shouted, "Boo!"

Shelpa leaped three feet in the air and landed on his backside with a painful bump.

"I can't believe you fell for that old gag!" said a marionette, slapping a palm against its forehead. It had gray shoes, gray pants, and a gray shirt, with its hands and face painted white. Strings extended into the sky from its head, hands, and knees.

Covering his heart with a hand, Shelpa felt the rapid *ta-dum ta-dum ta-dum* of its beating. "What gag?"

"Have you ever heard of Jack-in-the-Box? Well, I'm *Not*-in-the-Box."

Shelpa's brow furrowed as he gazed at the box and then back at the marionette. "I'm looking for the king."

"Of course you are. Why else would you be here? Everybody wants a question answered by the King Who Can't Laugh."

"Why's he called the King Who Can't Laugh?"

"Infinite wisdom has its price, my friend. After all, if you knew everything and everybody, if there were no more mysteries to solve, if every secret was known and every surprise as evident as your own arm, what wonder would remain to amuse you? What charm would the world have? The king's lonely and miserable, and if anyone can make him laugh, he'll celebrate with a feast."

"Food?"

"Not just food, my friend, but a feast, at the end of which he'll answer any one of your questions! But be warned: clowns, comedians, fools, and even jesters have tried to make him laugh, and so far . . . *all have failed to get even a snicker.*"

Shelpa began to glow intensely, imagining the king laughing and rewarding him with the knowledge of where Smiley was. "And what happens if I can't make him laugh?"

The marionette reached into the box and flipped a switch. The drawbridge creaked down from the castle and thudded against the ground. "Fail . . . and he will have your head."

Two shoes stepped out from the castle and crossed the drawbridge, twirling batons with their laces and leading a parade of flags, trumpets, and banging drums. Before Shelpa could object, they surrounded him and marched him across the bridge.

CHAPTER 12

THE PARADE BROUGHT Shelpa into a large room
with white drapes covering the walls and an elaborate tile
mosaic on the floor. The shoes led him across the floor
and through a hallway, at the end of which a stairway
wrapped around the inside of a tower. Here the shoes
stopped and took turns kicking Shelpa up the steps. One
after the other, they booted him in the behind until he
found himself at the top of the stairs, standing in front of
a door that looked and smelled like white chocolate. No
hinges connected the door to a frame, and Shelpa found
no knob to turn and nothing to push or pull. So he took
a bite, and several others, and then he broke off pieces
with his hands until he had made a hole big enough to
squeeze through.

He stepped into a huge room. The floor, ceiling,
and walls were made of white chocolate and decorated

with colorful jellybeans and jawbreakers. A rock-candy chandelier hung from the center of the ceiling, each of its arms bearing a caramel candlestick. A pink bubble-gum canopy—suspended between two candy-cane columns—was hanging above a throne made of marshmallows. A red carpet ran from the foot of the throne, down several steps, and across the room, where it ended at Shelpa's feet.

Shelpa marched across the carpet and stopped at the foot of the steps. Seated on the throne was the king. He had a long beard, and he was wearing a white robe and a sparkling gold crown. His eyes looked small and sinister.

"Next time, knock," he said, and laughed.

"I thought you can't laugh," Shelpa said.

"Of course I can laugh. I laugh all the time, whenever I want. But *you* can't make me laugh."

"I can try."

A grin spread across the king's face as his nostrils flared. "Good luck," he said. Then his face froze as hard as a fist.

Shelpa's lips pressed together as he climbed the steps to the throne, wondering what he could do to make the king laugh. Stuffing his hands in his hip pockets, he felt the purple feather he had caught in the air in front of Big Toe Hotel. He pulled it out, stopped in front of the king, and angled the feather below the king's chin.

The king held his breath, and began to redden, but Shelpa waited until he was as purple as the feather. Then, after blowing out his breath, the king said, "What are you waiting for? Do something!"

So Shelpa tapped the king's nose with the feather's tip, poked it inside his ear, and tickled his cheeks and chin. And the king laughed. He laughed so hard that Shelpa could see inside his mouth to the back of his throat. That made Shelpa laugh, and the entire chamber echoed with their hysterical laughter.

CHAPTER 13

AFTER THE KING recovered, he shook Shelpa's hand with a crushing grip.

"Congratulations, my friend! I haven't laughed like that in hours. Now follow me. I'll give you a tour of my castle."

"Could I ask my question first? It's urgent."

The king slapped Shelpa on the back, took his arm, and pulled him along. "You'll have time for your question after the feast. Follow me."

The king guided Shelpa into a gallery whose walls were covered with pictures painted by the monarch's most prized possession: a ruby that painted itself in various poses. The ruby's red hue reminded Shelpa of Smiley, and he wondered where she could be and if the king could help him find her.

The king indicated paintings of the ruby sitting, standing, walking, running through deserts and forests, and climbing hills and mountains. In one, the ruby was stepping over an ocean; in another, it was swallowing a star. An oval painting showed the ruby twirling a hoop around its waist, and a square one had the ruby balancing a jar of honey on its head. A swarm of bees surrounded the jar in a cloud of shimmering wings. Shelpa fidgeted, shifting his weight from one leg to the other as the king explained the history and composition of each painting. He discussed perspectives and proportions and interpreted the underlying meaning of each and every painting.

From there, the king led Shelpa down a flight of stairs and past a watchtower. They went up a ramp, crossed a courtyard, and entered a large chamber. In one corner, Shelpa saw two empty suits of armor shoving one another back and forth, trying to avoid standing under a vat of boiling oil.

"You first," one of them said.

"No, you first."

"No, I insist. *You* first!"

The king thrust out his chest. "Welcome to the Hall of Arms. My engineers are the best in the land. Look there!" The king pointed toward another corner of the room, where a bow was aiming an arrow at an apple on a table. The apple was shouting, "Higher! Lower! More to the right! A little to the left! Careful, or you might miss the table and hit *me!*"

Looking around the room, Shelpa saw a catapult about to launch a boulder through the window at a distant brick wall. Suddenly, the boulder screamed, "Wait a minute! What if the wall wins?" He also saw swords fighting in a craze of sparks, determined to break or be broken, and a battering ram holding its head and saying, "I've got a splitting headache!"

The castle was huge and had numerous halls, terraces, flights of stairs, and tapestries. Anxious to ask his question and resume his search for Smiley, Shelpa had a hard time concentrating as the tour dragged on.

He was desperate when, finally, the tour ended in a banquet room with doors of all shapes and sizes. He could see hundreds of doors, not only on the walls but on the floor and ceiling, too. Shelpa and the king sat at either end of a table that stretched across the room, so far apart they had to yell to communicate.

Cupping his hands around his mouth, the king screamed, "Are you ready?"

Shelpa scooted his chair forward. "Whenever you are!"

Reaching to his right, the king lifted a bell and rang it. Then he exchanged the bell for a knife and fork, which he gripped with the concentration of a matador in a bullfight, as servants entered through every door. They carried plates of pancakes with sliced bananas and coconut shavings, slabs of mozzarella sandwiched between juicy tomatoes, a platter of skewer kebabs, oodles of noodles, piles of garlic cheese bread, mashed potatoes, tacos, burritos, borscht, and a pumpkin pie.

The king forked up stacks of pancakes with one hand and gobbled them down, while using his other hand to stuff his face with slices of garlic cheese bread.

"Your Majesty," Shelpa shouted down the table as he spooned a tomato onto his plate, "do you eat like this all the time?"

"What?" the king yelled through a mouthful of crumbs. "You mean this snack?"

Shelpa ate some noodles. Then he wiped his mouth with a napkin and shouted, "Your Majesty? May I ask my question now?"

The king was cramming a dozen tacos into his mouth. He shook his head while gulping them down.

A short while later, after devouring the pie and his eighteenth bowl of borscht, the king started to wobble in his seat and stare at dust particles floating in front of his face.

Recognizing his last chance, Shelpa yelled, "Your Majesty? What about now? Could I ask my question?"

The king's head teetered back and forth as he slurred his words. "Yeth, of courthe."

"I'm looking for a friend, a flower. We were on the beach, and then she wandered into the forest, and I haven't seen her since. Where can I find her?"

"Oh, that'th eathy." The king raised his arm and pointed out the window. "Innda foretht. She'th innda thicket widda wathpth." Then he fell forward into the dish of potatoes.

Shelpa stared down at his hands and shook his head. He had not understood. He felt his sense of guilt and regret return like a herd of stampeding elephants. Then, as if on cue, a servant appeared, setting a bowl of vanilla ice cream on the table in front of him.

Yes! Shelpa thought. *My favorite!*

He could not resist ice cream. He checked his spoon for eyes or other signs of life. Finding none, he grabbed its handle and sunk its tip into the ice cream. The metal clanked against something solid. Shelpa fished the object out of the bowl and wiped it off with a napkin. It was shaped like a regular door key, but it was crumbly and rough, like a cookie. He had to squint to read the words along its shaft: FIRST KEY. He shrugged his shoulders, then slipped the cookie key into his chest pocket and zipped it shut. Returning his attention to the ice cream, he poked the spoon into other parts of the bowl. No more keys.

After finishing the ice cream, Shelpa stood up and looked around the room. He wondered which of the hundreds of doors would lead him back to the forest.

Oh boy, he thought. *This may take a while.*

CHAPTER 14

SHELPA LEFT THE king sleeping and tried one door after another, looking for a way out of the banquet room. Finally, he found a door that opened onto a narrow path, which Shelpa followed until he reached a tangled thicket. He struggled through, sidestepping large rocks, potholes, and puddles. The Xyzyx still looked sick, its face flushed and its eyes watery. It had chapped lips and a pained expression. Judging by its position in the sky, Shelpa figured a few hours had passed since he and Smiley had left the beach.

If I ever get out of this forest alive, he thought, *my parents are going to kill me.*

Still puzzling over the king's slurred words, he wondered where to go. He found a path that led out of the thicket and sloped up a hill, and he followed it in hopes of spotting Smiley, or signs of her passing, from above.

Layers of vegetation cushioned the ground, hushing his footsteps as he slipped through blue grass and feathery weeds. Here the air was invigorating and the forest alive with rustling leaves and crawling insects. Shelpa could see birds with fluffy wings and bushy tails perched on the boughs of trees. They entertained themselves by making music with their horn-shaped beaks. One of the birds leaped off a limb and darted into the air. Flapping its wings furiously, it nose-dived while blasting a melody of toots, then returned to its tree.

Shelpa was huffing and puffing by the time he reached the top of the hill, which was treeless and covered with short blades of blue grass. The sky was orange with purple streaks of clouds, a colorful contrast to the blue-grassed wilderness that swept down before him and extended up and over slopes. Beyond a stretch of trees and a meandering creek, he saw the brown mountain again and, at its foot, a trail that ended at what looked like a white-and-red cottage.

Shelpa followed the path over the hilltop as it swung around and descended a rocky slope. At the bottom of the hill, he found a spot where the path divided. Gazing along the route that swept off to the right, he saw the same thicket with wasps and a green mist fogging the air that he had seen after he left the beach.

Can't be, he thought, and his heart thumped in his

throat as a flash of red emerged from the mist like a ghost from thin air. *Is that really her,* he wondered, *or is the Xyzyx playing tricks on my eyes?*

Squinting against the light, Shelpa cracked his knuckles and flexed his fingers. It was Smiley coming up the path, her blossom bobbing on her stem. When she got near, Shelpa folded his arms across his chest and cleared his throat.

Smiley looked up. "You're here!" She rushed over and hugged him. "How wonderful! Don't you just love it here? And what about those signs insisting we stay out? Ridiculous, right? This forest is as tame as a turtle."

Shelpa kept his arms crossed and stood straight and stiff.

Smiley let go. She stepped back and looked at him.

Then he exploded. "Are you some kind of a crackpot? This forest is wacko. I could have been killed. You, too! We've got to get back to the beach. Immediately!"

Smiley pursed her lips. "Okay, calm down. First of all, we can't go back. Haven't you noticed?" Smiley pointed a leaf over Shelpa's shoulder.

Shelpa opened his mouth to protest, but then stopped and turned around. A sheer cliff had replaced the slope he had just descended. Staring at the ground, he nodded. "That's right. I forgot. The hat mentioned not being able to go back."

Smiley's blossom tilted to the side. "What hat?"

"Some sombrero I met on the way. It was hitchhiking, so I gave it a ride."

Smiley clicked her tongue. "Making friends in the forest, huh? Sounds like you've been having fun."

"Yeah, well, I wouldn't exactly call the hat a friend, and I certainly haven't been having fun. I've been looking for you. I was worried. I can't even imagine what our parents are going through and how much trouble I'm going to be in when we get back. *If* we get back. Where have you been?"

Just then, a bumblebee appeared, attracted to Smiley's scent. Tickled by the bee's buzz, Smiley waited until the bee had finished pollinating her. After it had flown out of sight, she sneezed. "Sorry. I'm allergic to fertilization." Then Smiley jerked a leaf in the direction she had come from. "I was over there."

Shelpa looked over toward the thicket, but all he saw was a wall of towering trees.

"Gee," Smiley said, "I guess it's gone now, too."

"When you first entered the forest, did you come to a clearing with two paths at the end?"

"Exactly."

"And you took the path with the wasps and green mist?"

"Right."

"Stinging wasps? Poisonous mist? You went that way?"

"Wasps are harmless if you leave them alone, and the mist wasn't poisonous. It was minty."

"So you were right there all this time?"

"Yep. I even took a nap. I woke up about ten minutes ago."

Shelpa cocked an eyebrow, curious and confused. In his mind, he went over the different routes they had traveled. He realized he must have taken the scenic route. "Well, we're in big trouble now," he said. "How are we going to get out?"

"Not by standing here."

"Of course not, but where should we go?"

Smiley tapped a root up and down on the path they

were standing on. "Looks like our choice is limited."

Shelpa gazed down the path and saw spiky plants, thorn-covered bushes, and trees whose branches stabbed like spears into the sky. "I don't like the looks of that."

"Oh, relax. We'll be fine."

The bee returned, attracted to Shelpa's glowing eyes. Shelpa waved an arm, and the bee flew between his fingers, circled his hand, and buzzed off. They watched the bee fly away, heading toward two boulders that stood on either side of the path. The bee dipped between the boulders, but as it passed, the boulders bashed against each together, squashing the bee flat between them.

Shelpa's forehead wrinkled as he looked at Smiley.

Leaves pressed to her lips, Smiley spoke in a whisper. "Yep, I saw it."

"What do you think it means?"

"That we'd better be *very* careful."

CHAPTER 15

SHELPA AND SMILEY slipped off the path to avoid the bee-smashing boulders, carefully navigating around the thorny bushes and sharp plants before returning to the trail. Soon the grass grew thick on either side and rose up high around them. As they walked, Shelpa told Smiley all about what had happened to him.

Grasshoppers leaped across the path and at times bounced off Shelpa or Smiley. Smiley shied away from them. She thought they were awful. After all, grasshoppers eat flowers. But Shelpa loved it when they hit his head or smacked into his body, and he howled, slapped his knee, or elbowed Smiley in the stem every time they did. One hopper got tangled in his hair and, struggling to escape, fell into one of his pockets. He pulled out the hopper and held it up to take a look at it. Its eyes had hundreds of bubbles with smaller eyes inside each one. He tried to show Smiley, but she turned away, disgusted. Shelpa laughed, glowing brighter as he clutched his sides, and then tossed the hopper into the weeds.

After following the path for several minutes, they came to a tree made of popcorn kernels. The tree started trembling as they approached, and when they neared, it blasted white puffy popcorn in every direction.

"It's afraid of you," Smiley said.

"Me? Why me?"

"Can't you tell? Your mishmash vibrations. They're the reason you fell off your surfboard, and they're also why that tack attacked you, the marionette scared the pookamajockas out of you, and the king wanted to chop off your head. Nothing like that has happened to me."

"I never said the king *wanted* to chop off my head. I only said he *could have.*"

"Watch this." Smiley picked up a piece of popcorn and put it in her mouth. "Mm, yum. You try one."

Shelpa grabbed a piece of popcorn off the ground by his foot. He tossed the popcorn into his mouth, and—*bang!*—the popcorn exploded. As Shelpa opened his mouth to speak, smoke billowed out. "Who'd have thought it could pop twice?"

"See what I'm saying? That's exactly it."

"What's exactly it?"

"The forest senses your anxious vibrations."

Shelpa brushed a strand of hair out of his eyes. "You think so?"

"Of course. When someone tosses a stone into a pond, the pond has to make space for the stone, just as the forest had to make room for you. A stone splashing into a pond makes ripples that spread out over the water, disturbing the reeds and the moss and any leaves floating on the pond's surface. And your awkward vibrations are disturbing the forest in a way that's causing your crazy encounters with tacks, sombreros, and cornball kings."

At that moment, a flash of lightning brightened the sky, and seconds later, a peal of thunder echoed across the forest. Shelpa's scalp tickled as static electricity raised the hair on his head. Chunky black clouds swept across the sky.

A thunderous roar followed another flash as drops of rain splattered the ground. Smiley spread her leaves and directed her blossom at the sky, relishing the fresh rainwater. But Shelpa cringed and looked around for cover. Remembering the cottage at the foot of the mountain, he grabbed one of Smiley's leaves and pulled her along.

"Come on. There's a cottage up ahead. We can wait out this storm in there."

Smiley yanked her leaf free. "I like the rain. You run for cover if you want."

"Oops. Sorry, I didn't think. But this looks like a serious thunderstorm. It could rip off your leaves and pluck out your petals."

Smiley eyed the sky, blinking against the raindrops. "You're probably right. Where'd you say this cottage was?"

CHAPTER 16

THE AIR TURNED warm and humid as the rain came down, and Shelpa and Smiley headed over a hill with grass like fox fur. Shelpa thought they might have missed a turn. He was hoping to connect to the trail he had seen from the top of the hill, but so far the path they were on was going in a different direction. Lightning flashed and thunder clapped as the path dipped down into a ravine. At the bottom, where the air smelled of wet leaves and old library books, their steps sank into muck. Smiley kept slipping. So Shelpa picked her up and, with a leaf around his neck, carried her over the swampy ground. She was so light that he imagined he was carrying a cloud.

Wind began to howl, driving the clouds across the sky as Shelpa carried Smiley over a bridge blanketed with pine needles. The path curved and then, after passing some bushes and heaps of pinecones, ended at the white cottage. The cottage had a red stripe wrapping around its walls like a ribbon, which was tied into a massive bow at the top of the roof. Behind the cottage, the brown mountain rose sharply into the sky.

Shelpa set Smiley down. Lightning zapped through the air, followed an instant later by booming thunder that seemed to rattle the bones in Shelpa's body. At the front door, they found a doormat with black borders and a yellow happy face embroidered on its surface.

The doormat greeted them. "Welcome! If nobody's inside, anyone can enter."

"Thanks!" Shelpa started to step forward but

stopped, feeling awkward.

"Go ahead," the doormat said. "That's what I'm here for."

"Thanks again!" Shelpa said, stepping gingerly.

"Yur wulcome," said the mat, its voice muffled by Shelpa's feet.

Shelpa licked his lips, then knocked. Nobody answered, so he knocked again, harder. After a minute without a response, he tried to turn the knob.

"Oh boy."

"What's the matter?" Smiley asked.

"It's locked."

Shelpa saw that Smiley was waiting patiently, and he wondered how she could stay calm in such a situation. He grabbed the doorknob and jiggled it back and forth. The knob broke off in his hand. Thunder rumbled like a landslide crashing down a mountain as he tossed the doorknob into a hedge.

Shelpa looked down at the doormat. "Any suggestions?"

"Giit uff mme," the mat said.

He stepped backward. "The knob broke. What do we do now?"

"The key's underneath me. But it's too late for that."

Shelpa looked around. "Is there a back door?"

"Nope."

"An open window I could crawl through?"

"Sorry."

Thinking, Shelpa massaged the knuckles of his right hand. The rain fell in slanting sheets, and lightning clawed down from the ceiling of black clouds. The wind howled, whipping leaves around as branches flailed back and forth. Suddenly, he had an idea. After backing up a step, he leaned back, and kicked the door. It did not budge.

"Let me try," Smiley said.

"Just a minute." Shelpa headed down the walk, turned to face the cottage, and sprinted toward the door.

Smiley hugged her shoulders, drew a deep breath, and winced as Shelpa hurled himself against the door and fell back with a thud. He stood on the doormat, massaging his elbow. Smiley gestured for him to move aside. She stepped forward, reached into the hole where the knob had been, and poked her leaf around. At the sound of a click, the door opened.

CHAPTER 17

DRIPPING WET, SHELPA and Smiley went in and closed the door. The light was dim, so Smiley tickled Shelpa until he shined enough to illuminate the entryway. Similar to the cottage's exterior, a red stripe circled the walls, spiraling toward the center of the ceiling and then curling into a bow to form a chandelier, which was giving off a reddish glow.

They stepped into a room where a fluffy green rug covered the floor, and two wicker chairs faced a stone fireplace. Blocks of wood and sticks were piled by one side of the fireplace, and stacks of newspaper by the other. Shelpa and Smiley sank into the chairs. Rain pattered on the roof.

Smiley was shivering. "I'm c-c-cold."

Shelpa scooted over to the fireplace. He grabbed several pages of newspaper, crumpled them up, and tossed them in. Finding a box of matches on the mantel, he struck one and lit the newspaper. He placed a handful of sticks on the burning paper, and once those were alight, he stacked three blocks of wood over the flames. Soon the fire was crackling.

Looking over at Smiley, he asked, "Are you okay sitting so close? The fire's not going to wilt you, is it?"

"No, I'm fine. Thanks."

Shelpa grabbed the poker from its hook by the fireplace and used it to move one of the pieces of wood closer to the heart of the fire. "By the way, there's something I didn't tell you before. I keep seeing words, four so far, and there's a blue kangaroo that puts them in places for me to find."

"What do the words say?"

"First there was 'clever,' then 'determined,' then 'courageous,' and finally 'rational.'"

"At least they're encouraging words."

"Also, the first time I saw the kangaroo, it poked my leg with its tail and then pointed up at the trees."

"Was there anything strange about the trees?"

Shelpa's eyes wandered around the room as if he might find the answer on the walls somewhere. "No, they were normal, ordinary trees with regular branches and leaves."

"One thing's for sure, you've got a wacky relationship with this forest, or maybe the whole planet. Listen, everything happens for a reason. You've just got to figure out what that reason is."

Shelpa blinked several times. "Really? You think *everything* happens for a reason?"

"Absolutely. On Pix, there's a theory called the Law of Loops. We believe a balance exists between nature and all things, and our vibrations affect that balance. Thoughts have vibrations. Words have stronger vibrations. Actions have the strongest vibrations of all. Just like the water cycle is a circle, and the food chain, too, your thoughts, words, and actions come back to you full circle. Everything operates in relation to everything else. That's why I think your nervous vibrations are causing these crazy encounters. They're upsetting the balance, which might explain why that kangaroo is writing those words."

Shelpa retrieved the poker and clutched its handle with both hands. "Seems too simple, doesn't it? I mean, if that was all there was to it, life would be easy, wouldn't it?"

"Exactly. Life on Pix *is* easy."

Shelpa said nothing. He put down the poker again and picked up a stick from the woodpile. He plucked a splinter off the stick and flicked it into the fire. He sat lost in thought, biting his bottom lip as his eyes glowed.

"What are you thinking about?" she asked, leaning toward the fire.

"I was trying to imagine what life on Pix must be like, and somehow that got me wondering what the universe would look like if everything was invisible."

"Well? What would it look like?"

"I don't know. That's what I was wondering."

The fire popped, and sparks swished upward through the air. Shelpa set aside the stick, grabbed another block of wood, and put it on the fire. Orange-tipped flames flicked at the wood.

"I'm thirsty," Smiley said.

"Wait here," Shelpa said, rising. "I'll check the kitchen."

She stood up. "That's all right. I'll come with you."

CHAPTER 18

SHELPA AND SMILEY crossed the entryway and went down a hall. Shelpa opened the first door and found the bathroom. Then, from farther along the hallway, he heard Smiley call, "Here it is!"

As he walked into the kitchen, he saw white cupboards above and below the sink, a refrigerator and freezer next to the stove, a blender by the oven, and an orange table and chairs. Gleaming as if recently mopped, the floor was made of white tiles divided by thin, gray lines. The ceiling and walls were made of glass with decals in each corner that read UNBREAKABLE. Outside, the storm was ripping plants out of the ground and raining balls of hail the size of fists.

Smiley was standing in front of the refrigerator, holding open the door and peering inside.

"What're you having?" Shelpa squeezed in beside her.

"Water." Smiley grabbed a bottle. "Want some?"

"Sure."

"Get some glasses."

Shelpa searched the cupboards. He found two glasses and set them on the table. As Smiley poured the water, Shelpa looked in the freezer. Reaching in, he moved some things around. "I can't believe this!"

"What?" Smiley asked.

"No ice cream, just a tray of ice cubes and a box of ice pops."

"You're funny."

"Not on purpose."

"Maybe not, but you are anyway."

Shelpa took the glass Smiley gave him. Then he closed the freezer and sat down, facing her. She stared through the wall, sipping her water as wind tore a branch off a tree and then smashed it into the glass inches from Smiley's face.

She flinched and crossed her roots. "If you could have one super power, what would it be?"

Shelpa moved his chair closer to the table. He rested his elbows on it and said, "You mean if I could see through walls, fly, or be invisible? Stuff like that?"

"Exactly."

Rubbing his chin with a knuckle, he looked through the ceiling at the lightning forking across the sky. "I'd like to be able to change the past, to unmake mistakes I've made."

Smiley put down her glass. "But then you wouldn't be you. Mistakes make us interesting. And everybody makes mistakes. The important thing is to learn from them and try not to make the same mistakes twice.

Then they're really just stepping-stones that lead to a better you."

Shelpa's head jerked back. "You think making mistakes is a good thing?"

"Not always, but making mistakes is inevitable, and learning from them is how you get experience and wisdom. That's what I meant when I told you about harmonizing your vibrations. If you regret a mistake, that fuels the negative energy inside you, which disturbs your vibrations. You need to accept your mistakes, like the pond that becomes calm again after making space for the stone."

Shelpa drummed his fingers on the tabletop. "Something else happened while I was looking for you." He unzipped his pocket and pulled out the cookie key, which he handed to Smiley.

She took the key in her leaf, touched its rough exterior, and then gave it back to him. "Where'd you get it?"

"From the king's castle. It was a gift, I think."

"Obviously, it opens something. A secret door? A magic wardrobe? A treasure chest?"

Shelpa raised his glass and finished his water in one gulp. He dropped the key back into his pocket and then stared at his hands, inspecting the whitish half-moons at the base of each fingernail. Outside, the wind battered the trees. Stripped of leaves, their branches whipped back and forth like strands of rope.

Smiley pushed a petal out of her face. "What do you think it's for?"

Shelpa gazed at his empty glass. "No idea."

"A blue kangaroo, mysterious words, and a key made out of a cookie. I have to admit, it's puzzling. It must mean *something.* Have you ever seen a blue kangaroo before?"

Shelpa's shine dimmed. He slipped his hands into his pockets. He leaned back in his chair and stared blankly at the air in front of his face. He started to speak but then stopped and looked out the window. Two rocks collided in midair, smashing to smithereens, and Shelpa shut his eyes as rock fragments rained down on the glass. When he spoke, his voice was faint. "I have, actually, but . . ." He reached forward and slid his empty glass to the left. A tear leaked from his eye, and he wiped it away.

"I'm sorry. I didn't mean—"

"No, it's okay. It's not your fault."

Smiley finished her water and stood up. "I'm cold. Let's go back to the fireplace."

Shelpa refilled his glass and gulped down the water. He put both glasses and the bottle in the sink, and they left the kitchen.

CHAPTER 19

BACK IN THE living room, they sat in the chairs, watching the wood burn. Occasionally, an ember would pop, shooting glowing streaks against the inside of the chimney.

We've got to get out of this forest and back to the beach before nightfall, Shelpa thought, *and we're stuck in this cottage as precious minutes pass. Why a monsoon when we're in such a rush?*

Using the poker, he pushed blocks of wood around the fireplace. Then he stabbed at some fading ashes. He put down the poker and grabbed a board, which he broke in half over his knee and tossed into the fire. Then he used the poker to arrange the wood, pushing embers into the middle and balancing both halves of the board over the flames.

"Comfortable?" he asked Smiley.

"Yep."

Hail pounded the roof as rain pelted the windows.

"What you said earlier about things happening for a reason, and my anxiety causing all these crazy encounters . . . If that's true, then this whole storm could be a reaction to what I'm thinking and how I feel."

"It's possible."

"That seems too simple to me. On Shine, things happen all the time without rhyme or reason. As far as I can tell, stuff happens just because it happens, and you have to live with the consequences, even if you don't like them, or if they're painful." The fire warmed Shelpa's face, reddening his cheeks. "But if you agree with the Law of Loops, then you'd have to admit that I'm trapped in this forest because of *your* actions, because *you* went into the forest."

Smiley's roots stiffened, and her leaves pressed flat on the seat of her chair. "It's my fault that *I'm* here. It's your fault that *you're* here."

"How can you say that? I wouldn't be here if *you* had listened to me."

Smiley lifted a leaf and opened her mouth to speak.

"No," Shelpa said, "from now on, you need to follow my directions. I'm in charge, and it's my responsibility to get us back to the beach."

"There you go again, Mr. Bossy. Okay, Sergeant Shelpa, whatever you say." Smiley sat up straight and saluted. Then, shaking her blossom, she leaned back in her chair.

Shelpa tossed another fresh log on the flames. "First of all, we're going to wait out this storm," he said, punctuating his words with a jab of his finger. "Then once it's over, we're going to get out of this crazy forest."

"This isn't the way to be a friend or to make a friend. I'm telling you this as a friend. Trust me. We'll both be better off as soon as you get it into your radiant head that I'm going to do whatever I want."

"No," Shelpa said, shaking his head. "Not this time. This time, I'm not taking my eyes off you. I'll sit on you if I have to. Once this storm's over, I'm going to pick you up and carry you back to the beach. I mean it."

Lips quivering, Smiley turned her blossom to look straight at Shelpa. "You can't force someone to be friends."

Shelpa grabbed the poker and shuffled the wood around in the fireplace. He pushed an unburned block of wood into the middle. "Nobody's forcing you to be friends. Besides, I've got enough friends."

"Fine. I'm leaving." Smiley stood up and started out of the room.

Shelpa's skin prickled. Shimmering with irritation, he hung the poker on a nail and grabbed Smiley by her stem. With her lips flattened, she jerked away, twisted out of his grip, and then turned and kicked his shin.

Shelpa blazed as bright as a forest fire. "Was that supposed to hurt? Kicking me with a root?"

"Never mind. You keep your hands to yourself. Being bossy is one thing, but nobody touches me without my permission. Got it?"

Grinding his teeth, Shelpa shined as bright as he ever had. "You do what I say! *I'm in charge!*" He was so luminous now that his eyes snapped shut against the brilliance of his own light. He groped around with his arms out, reaching with his fingers. "Boy oh boy, now you've done it! I can't even see myself!"

There was silence for several seconds, and then Shelpa heard the door open. He felt a blast of cold air as the door slammed shut. Still blinded by his own brightness, he lurched forward, tripped on the leg of his chair, and fell on the rug. He rolled onto his back and tried to lessen his glow by inhaling and exhaling slowly, counting to three between each breath. When he had reduced his shine enough to crack open his eyes, he leaped to his feet and raced to the door. He could not see her anywhere, and he shook his fist in the air, blood surging through his veins.

"Smiley! Come back!"

CHAPTER 20

SHELPA STOOD IN front of the cottage, fuming. Smiley was nowhere to be seen. She could have gone in any direction. The storm had passed, but raindrops still fell on the ground, which was covered with shredded leaves and broken twigs. Trees, wet and glistening, swayed in the lingering breeze.

Shelpa swallowed hard and then screamed again. "Smiley! Where are you?" He cocked an ear but heard nothing. He wondered what to do.

If I go left, and she went right, he thought, *that's it. I'll never find her.*

As he stood, wringing his hands, he heard a sawing sound coming from behind the cottage, and followed it around to the back. Here the mountain loomed overhead, and he stared up to where its summit disappeared into the clouds, only now realizing that the entire mountain was made of wood. Instead of plants, trees, rocks, and rivers, he saw extraordinarily realistic carved and painted boards. The wood was nailed, screwed, glued, and roped together like a giant jungle gym. Some of its peaks were platforms, and bridges spanned vast areas of empty space, linking several ridges together.

Shelpa heard more sawing and some hammering. He followed the sounds up a narrow plank. After hiking over a ramp, he looped around a curve and climbed a steep slope. Around another corner, he just about ran into a man on a ladder, toothpick dangling from his mouth, who was using a mallet to hammer a sign onto two upright boards. His pants and shirt were ragged, and a stained and tattered cap covered his head. At each blow of the mallet, he grunted as if he were straining himself.

"Excuse me," Shelpa said.

The man stopped and stared down with grainy eyes and knotted lips. Shelpa was stunned to realize that the man was made of wood. Ball joints joined his limbs, allowing his elbows, knees, and neck to bend and turn, and his clothes, hat, and face seemed to have been carved by a master craftsman. With a voice like sandpaper scraping tree bark, he asked, "What d'ya want?"

Shelpa stared, speechless. He blinked several times and then asked, "By any chance have you seen a red flower around here?"

"Ya won't find any flowers here, not real ones anyway."

"I mean a flower who, uh, walks and . . . talks."

Gritting his chiseled teeth and staring hard at Shelpa, he said, "Look, pal, I got lots of signs to post. Supposed to have this one up minutes ago. Now I gotta answer crazy questions, too? You wanna ask questions, you go ask the light spirit, though it's a long way to reach him, and you can find him only by not looking." The man turned back to his work, raised the mallet, and took one final crack at the sign. Then he hopped down, grabbed his ladder, and rushed off. Shelpa watched him go, the mallet swinging at his side, and then looked up at the sign, which read MOUNT TIMBER.

"Here goes nothing," Shelpa said as he decided to try once again to spot Smiley from higher ground. He climbed Mount Timber for a quarter of an hour, his first goal being a platform he could see not too far above. Sweat-soaked, with his back aching, he scaled a steep chute, skirting the edge of a vertical drop-off that had nails protruding from its sides at different heights and angles.

The air was hot and muggy. Shelpa was about to stop and rest in the shade of a tree house, but then the way leveled out and brought him to the platform, which turned out also to be a crossroads. Planked paths headed in various directions, and a signpost in the middle read:

Here ↑
←There
Where →
←↑ Right Here
Over There →↓
↑← This Way
That Way ↓
←↓ Any Way
What Way ↓ →
←↑→↓ Which Way
A Way → ↓ ←↑
←↑→↓ The Way

Shelpa shook his head, amused by the sign. Then, as he looked down each path, sawdust started falling from the clouds, blinding him. He accidentally inhaled some, gagging as it clogged his windpipe. Shielding his eyes with one hand and pursing his lips, he headed along a path to his right in search of shelter.

The grains of sawdust solidified when they reached the ground, forming wooden walls and then roofs, and fenced Shelpa into a maze. He kept moving. His shine illuminated the way as he went, but each path split into multiple branches. Choosing turns by instinct, he followed those that seemed to go down, but found they led him only higher. At a fork, he selected a tunnel that angled upward, hoping to go down, but as the way curved left and the slope evened out, he came to a dead end. He turned to go back, but a new wall blocked his way. Shelpa was trapped!

CHAPTER 21

SHELPA TOOK A DEEP breath and tried to stay
calm. He was standing in a room with no exits. From
the inside, it looked like a large wooden crate. He saw
matchsticks on the ground.

Maybe I can burn my way out of here, he thought.

He picked up a match and struck its tip against the
wall. Then he held the flame up to the ceiling, which caught
fire so abruptly that Shelpa leaped back and dropped the
match. In a burst of flashes and hissing sparks, other matches
ignited, and flames shot up around him. He jumped up and
down to stomp out the fire on the floor as flames climbed
the walls and swallowed the ceiling. Shelpa backed away
from the blistering heat and pressed against a wall as the
air filled with choking smoke. As the fire swept closer, he
closed his eyes against the swirling smoke, dropped to his
knees, and cradled his head. He tried to think of an idea,

any idea, to save his life, and as he did, he heard loud, ringing laughter.

Shelpa sat up and wiped his teary eyes. The fire was confined to a lightbulb floating above his head. The bulb illuminated the box's interior—and laughed from a mouth that stretched across the surface of its glass.

It spoke with a sizzling voice. "Trying to think of an idea to save yourself is a good start, but you can do better than that, I think."

Shelpa's eyebrows slanted. "Are you the light spirit?"

The bulb brightened as two glowing eyes appeared above its mouth. "No, I'm not the light spirit. I'm your thoughts made physical."

Now a nose appeared between the eyes.

Shelpa's jaw dropped. "What do you mean?"

"I'm part of your mind. I know everything you know, and I become whatever you're thinking. I may become a skateboard to ride or a snowy slope to ski down. Occasionally, I turn into a book to read, some cotton candy to eat, or a brand-new videogame to play. This isn't the first time I've been a lightbulb. Anyway, what can I do for you?"

Shelpa shook with excitement, thinking the bulb could help him find Smiley.

As if reading his mind, the bulb said, "Sorry, I can't help you with her. I can only help you to help yourself."

"Can you at least point me in the right direction?"

"If you don't know, I don't know, either. But I *might* be able to tell you what you already know but refuse to realize."

"Which is?"

"That you only *think* you're trapped. In fact, most problems exist only in your mind."

"Well, I can't go forward or back, or right or left. So what does that leave me?"

"What do *you* think?"

Shelpa looked up at the charred ceiling and then down at the blackened floor. "You mean up or . . . down?"

"See that? Sometimes thinking *outside* the box solves your most pressing problems."

"But how? There are no doors. No windows. No way out."

"Every problem has a solution. You only need to think the right way."

"So?"

"So . . . I've already said. I become whatever you *think,* so think constructively, and be specific."

Shelpa remembered the sawing sound that had drawn him to the mountain, and imagined a handsaw.

"That's better!" The lightbulb vanished in a wisp of smoke, leaving a saw in its place. Shelpa picked up the saw and gripped the handle firmly. The ceiling was too high for him to cut a hole and then climb through, so he started sawing into the floor. He made a square big enough to squeeze through and dropped the saw into one of his pockets. As he was sticking his legs into the opening he heard the pattering hops of what he believed to be the kangaroo. Then he saw a word carved into the wood: PRACTICAL.

CHAPTER 22

SHELPA DROPPED INTO a narrow tunnel. The ceiling was low, and the air made his mouth dry. He set off along the passage, his shining illuminating the stone walls a few feet ahead and the rocks scattered over the ground.

He splashed through a puddle, shuffled around a pothole, and then squeezed through an area constricted by outcroppings and heaps of crumbled boulders. While stepping around a gap on one side of the passage, he walked into something stiff but springy. Shelpa tried to back away but found he was glued to some sort of mesh. His right arm was free, but the rest of him was stuck. He tried to twist his left arm or bend a leg to break free, but his efforts were useless. The threads and glue held fast. All around him, he saw silky strands covering the tunnel's circumference. He was entangled in a spiderweb.

He heard something scuffling across the stone above his head as a droning voice said, "Mmmmussst be mmmy lunchtimmmmmmmme."

Shelpa went numb. "Who's there?"

A form the size of Shelpa's head crept into sight, clinging to the ceiling with long, spindly legs. Its eyes were black bubbles, and two fangs jutted down from its mouth. As the spider shifted from the ceiling to the wall and then climbed onto the web, Shelpa noticed a blood-red hourglass shape on its stomach.

His heartbeat thrashed in his ears as the spider advanced.

"Oh yesssss. A tasssty mmmmorsssel you'll mmmake."

Shelpa fought to pull himself free from the threads, sending vibrations rippling through the web.

The black widow's eyes bulged. "Tremmmbling mmm-makessss mmmmy mmmeal mmuch lessssss pleasurable. Pleassse don't." One of its legs stroked Shelpa's throat. "I prefer prey that acceptsss itsss fate with hummmmility."

Shelpa remembered the fire he had made, and wished he had a match. He tried to think one into existence, but nothing happened. Then he remembered the handsaw in his pocket. His right hand was near its handle. Trying to distract the arachnid, he asked, "Are you going to eat me?"

"Goodnessssss no. That'sss not mmmmy mmmethod.

I'mmmm going to nip you on the neck. Don't worry. It won't hurt . . . mmmmuch."

"And then?" Shelpa moved his arm toward his pocket. "What happens after that?"

"Never mmmind. You'd rather not know."

"No, please. Tell me everything."

The spider noticed Shelpa reaching into his pocket.

It scuttled down toward his hand. "Sssssommething in there?"

Shelpa yanked out the saw and thrust his arm upward, plunging the toothed edge into the spider's abdomen. It popped as if filled with air, and the spider flew around the tunnel like a deflating balloon as guts and green goo sprayed the walls.

Shelpa hacked through the web's strands and freed himself. He wanted to run and hide, but he stayed where he was, trying to gather his wits. He was afraid he would run into another web. As his nerves settled, he saw a shadow dart out of sight. The kangaroo! He took several steps in its direction, searching for the word it had left. He found the word etched into the wall: LEVELHEADED. His heart raced with gratification at the sight of it.

As he turned away, he heard the echoing sound of water flowing. He moved toward the sound, and after a short distance, the tunnel opened into a chamber. A stream flowed through it, leaving through a crevice in the wall and disappearing into darkness.

That's the way out, he thought, *but I need to find some sort of boat.*

Near the stream bank, he saw a barrel filled with debris. He tipped it over and dumped out woodchips, sawdust, and balls of crumpled paper. Then he rolled the empty barrel into the stream, where the awkward vessel wobbled and tugged against the current.

Shelpa climbed in and shoved off. While he floated downstream, he started to wonder about the light spirit. How could he find someone he could not look for?

CHAPTER 23

SHELPA HAD BEEN tipping and bobbing in the barrel for several minutes when he heard the sound of a gushing torrent. Alarmed, he shined brighter as the current carried him along faster and the roar increased. He could see the water churning and frothing, and looking ahead, he spotted a whirlpool. He gripped the barrel's sides, bracing himself, and then held his breath and squeezed his eyes shut as he felt the barrel lurch downward. The vortex swallowed the barrel whole and whirled it around and around.

Shelpa was wrenched out of the barrel, and the handsaw out of his pocket. He opened his eyes, worried that the saw's blade would slash him as they both spun in circles, but luckily the saw was sucked out of sight, while Shelpa was flung out of the whirlpool into calmer water.

Shelpa soon realized that not only could he see clearly underwater, he could also breathe the water like air. Before long, he was floating above a coral reef. He swam toward what looked like a shoreline, passing starfish, sea anemone, jellyfish, and octopuses. But when the reef ended, the ocean floor dipped down, and he found himself swimming through a kelp bed he had mistaken for land. Slimy kelp fronds brushed his arms and legs. Then, as he came out the other side, he saw a blue city shimmering in the distance.

As he neared, he noticed a throng of sea creatures waiting to greet someone. Many were gliding back and forth, waving WE LOVE YOU, PAOLINO! banners. A leaflet floated past Shelpa's face, and he read the words at the top: APPEARING TONIGHT FOR THE FIRST OF FIVE PERFORMANCES, THE GREAT PAOLINO! The photograph below the name looked like Shelpa, though the forehead was flatter and the earlobes longer.

As cheers and shouts gurgled and bodies pressed forward, a squadron of great white sharks surrounded Shelpa. The sharks attacked anyone who came too near, and gobbled several guppies. A band started playing, beating drums and blasting trombones and trumpets.

Shelpa tried to raise his voice above the din of the band and screaming fans. "Listen, uh, somebody! I'm not who you think I am!"

A stingray appeared and shepherded Shelpa along while yelling, "Welcome to Sapphire City, Paolino, sir! We are thrilled to have you here! You're much later than we expected, so we'll have to hurry if you're going to be ready for your first performance. If you'll please come with me, your transportation is right this way!" With the sharks leading, the stingray guided Shelpa through the crowd as the band followed behind them.

After swimming above a sapphire avenue, they came to an area sectioned off by strands of seaweed and patrolled by hammerheads. The stingray lifted a strand, allowed Shelpa to pass beneath, and then motioned for him to sit inside a giant oyster shell. As he sat down, Shelpa discovered the interior was padded with sponges.

He turned to the stingray. "I'm really sorry, but I think you've confused m—"

"No no no, *I'm* sorry! I forgot you prefer kelp cushions." The stingray waved a fin, and in an instant the sponges had been removed and replaced by layers of kelp.

The stingray snapped its tail, signaling a team of seahorses that pulled the shell through clouds of goldfish confetti and rows of coral skyscrapers. The celebration raged all around: crabs and lobsters clicked their claws, and eels wiggled frantically. Every sea creature fought for a view of Shelpa.

The stingray swam near Shelpa's ear. "Believe it or not, most of the city is sculpted from a single sapphire. The only exceptions are the coral skyscrapers and that seashell in the middle." The stingray pointed to a colossal white seashell at the far end of the avenue. "That's our celebrated auditorium, designed by Sapphire City's most renowned architect, Eduardo Angelino. And that's where you'll be performing for the next five nights."

Shelpa could see neon letters flashing on a marquee above its entrance, spelling out SEASHELL OPERA HALL.

"Listen, sir," Shelpa said, again trying to speak above

the clamor of honking tubas and bashing tambourines, "I'm not who you think I am. There's been a mistake."

"A break? Of course, as many as you like. After all, you're the star!"

The band continued to play, the masses to cheer, and confetti to float as they followed the avenue leading toward the seashell. The pageant was like nothing Shelpa had ever experienced, let alone been the center of. But the crowd thought they were applauding Paolino, not Shelpa, and Shelpa worried what would happen when they realized who he really was. Imagining what might occur if he exposed himself before this frenzied multitude, he decided not to say anything until he could explain the misunderstanding under safer circumstances.

At that moment, a sea turtle dashed forward, wanting to shake Shelpa's hand, request an autograph, or perhaps just adore him. A great white chased the sea turtle away, and a catfish took advantage to grab at Shelpa's overalls and pull the purple feather out of his pocket. The catfish darted away with the prize trailing from its mouth.

Arriving at the auditorium, the seahorses pulled up to the curb. Sea creatures swarmed the entrance area, chanting, "Pao-lin-o! Pao-lin-o!" They shoved, pinched, and pushed each other back and forth as they struggled to peep at Shelpa. A dolphin, gray except for his coffee-brown eyes and milk-white belly, was waiting by the entrance. His round, protruding nose bobbed up and down as he swam over and then circled the oyster shell.

"Welcome, welcome, welcome," he said. "We're so glad you could come. Better late than never, as they say, right? My name is Phineas, and I'm honored, sir. Truly honored." Phineas bowed. "Sorry to bother you, but I've been waiting so long, and I'm curious to know: What's your favorite song to sing? How do you hit those high notes? And do you exercise your diaphragm, and if so, how often?"

Shelpa's head buzzed as if filled with flies. He was supposed to sing, but he did not know what, and worse, he did not know how. He also had no idea how to answer these questions as if he were Paolino. He pressed his palms together as if in prayer. "Listen, Phineas, I'm not the Great Paolino. Somehow everybody's mixed me up with him."

The dolphin's jaw tightened. He responded in a whisper. "Do you realize how many clams we'll lose if we cancel the shows? Not to mention the mayhem. You're going to have to play along for now. Follow me." With a devious wink of an eye and a wave of his flipper, Phineas ushered Shelpa through a side door that led to the auditorium's backstage area. The crowd continued to scream as the doors slammed shut behind them.

CHAPTER 24

PHINEAS LED SHELPA through a circular passageway toward the dressing room. "As the event coordinator, I insist you pretend to be the Great Paolino. If my boss finds out there's been another mix-up, I'll be out of a job. Unless the real Paolino arrives in time, *you'll* be performing."

A starfish was clinging to the center of the dressing-room door. As they approached, the starfish smiled at both Phineas and Shelpa. Turning from pink to purple, the sea creature said, "Excuse me, Mr. Paolino, sir. Would you mind signing an autograph for my son?"

Shelpa felt sick to his stomach and scratched his neck nervously. "N-not at all."

Beaming, the starfish handed the spine of a sea urchin and a flat piece of coral to Shelpa. As Shelpa carved his assumed name, the starfish peeked over his shoulder.

Shelpa noticed the starfish's pupils widen as he handed back the autograph. After tucking away the materials, the starfish crawled over to the knob and opened the door. Phineas and Shelpa floated inside.

Though the room was compact, mirrors on the walls, floor, and ceiling made the surroundings seem to expand infinitely in every direction. Snail shells filled with worms rested atop a table in the far corner. There was a closet, a sink and counter, and another door on the far wall. Makeup, hairpins, masks, wigs, and jewelry filled buckets under the sink.

Phineas swam to the closet. "All the costumes are in here." He slid the door aside, revealing various outfits. Then his voice dropped. "Stay here. Say nothing to nobody."

Shelpa cleared his throat as he fingered the sleeve of a rubber suit with green quills lining the arms and legs. "I'm not going anywhere."

Phineas smiled suspiciously, wrinkles circling his eyes. After he left the room, the starfish shut the door.

Shelpa paced back and forth, seeing himself reflected from every angle all over the room. He saw a worried look on his face—his brow was furrowed and his lips pressed tight. This one reflection repeating itself over and over again reminded him of what Smiley had said about his anxious vibrations.

He walked over to the far wall and tried to open the second door. It was locked. So Shelpa continued to pace the room, hoping the real Paolino would arrive and save him from disaster. He was at his wit's end when Phineas returned with two great whites at his side.

"What? No costume?" Phineas screwed up his face. "Chomp! Muncher! You know the routine."

One of the sharks swam to the closet and returned with a costume. Together, the two sharks muscled Shelpa into it. Looking in the mirror, he could see he was dressed from head to toe in an oversized suit whose sleeves and legs ballooned out as if inflated. A massive ruffled collar framed his neck, tilting upward like an upside-down bell around his head.

Phineas nudged Shelpa through the door and along the passageway. Nearing the stage, Shelpa heard an echoing voice announce, "Swimmers, floaters, and bottom feeders, welcome to Seashell Opera Hall. Tonight, we are honored to present . . . *the Great Paolino!*"

The thunderous buzz of cheers and applause was deafening as Phineas shoved Shelpa onto the stage, whose glossy blue sheen was polished as smooth as a pearl. The crowd waved and wiggled and thrashed about, and several seals fainted at the sight of him and had to be carried away by manta rays.

Shelpa was breathless. He felt a weight like a

bowling ball in his stomach. He was shocked to see so many sea creatures filling the auditorium. Between all the bubbles and confusion, there seemed to be more bodies than seats.

His vision blurred as the spotlight came on, and he grabbed the microphone that stood in front of him. The crowd fell silent as Shelpa positioned his mouth near the microphone. He glanced at Phineas, who was now seated in the first row between Chomp and Muncher. Phineas nodded his head and narrowed his eyes. Shelpa gulped and glanced around at the mob of sea creatures staring with anticipation and delight, their complete attention fixed on him.

His lips started trembling as he cleared his throat and laughed nervously. Then, finally, he spoke. "E-e-excuse me, everyone, b-but there's been a mistake. I'm not the Great Paolino. My n-name is Shelpa, and I'm sorry, but there's no way I c-can sing tonight! Heck, I can't even *hum* in tune!"

He heard hushed voices and the sounds of sea creatures squirming in their seats as they struggled to grasp his words. Shelpa glanced at Phineas, who was staring at him, dumbfounded, bubbles forming in the corners of his mouth.

Then, from a seat near the back of the auditorium, a gurgling voice screamed, "We've been had! Get him!"

In a fit of nerves, Shelpa bolted backstage. He swam like crazy until he reached the dressing-room door. He knocked the starfish aside and jerked open the door, yanking it shut behind him. After locking the door, he pulled off the costume in one swift motion and left it in a heap on the floor. Seconds later, someone pounded hard, and an unfamiliar voice shouted, "Listen, you, whoever you are, open the door, now!"

The knob jiggled as Shelpa raced toward the second door at the opposite end of the room. He remembered how Smiley had opened the cottage door, and he tried to break off the knob, but it was too strong. Then, remembering a trick he had seen his dad do, Shelpa swam to the closet and grabbed a wire hanger. He returned to the door, bent the hanger's hook into a loop, and jammed the loop into the gap between the door and the frame, right where the lock was. He settled the loop against the latch, fiddling with the wire while pushing and pulling on the door.

Behind him, the hammering on the first door continued. "Listen, you, the game is up! Come on outta there!"

With nerves raw and knees buckling, he gripped the hanger more firmly and scraped the loop in and out while wiggling the knob. Incredibly, the second door popped open.

Shelpa pressed a palm to his heart as he stared outside, into a realm of air. He saw a lush meadow under an apple-red sky. Orange and blue butterflies fluttered above emerald-green grass spotted with flowers. In the center of the meadow, a hundred feet away, an elevator shaft rose into the air.

Just then, a loud bang jolted the first door, rattling the door in its frame. "That's good, Whopper! Another crack like that oughta do! You're in trouble now, kid! Here we come!"

Shelpa yelled across the room, "It's not my fault! I told the truth, but no one would listen to me!"

At that moment, written in lipstick on the mirror, he noticed the word HONEST. Shelpa flung up his arms, forming a V for victory, and then popped out of the watery element and into fresh air.

CHAPTER 25

NO LONGER NEEDING to swim, Shelpa charged toward the elevator. As he got closer, however, he felt fainter and fainter. The flowers' perfume was so potent that it numbed his mind. He staggered forward, struggling to remain conscious. He thought he saw a flower wink at him, while another one waved. Someone shouted, and though the words seemed measured and remote, he heard, "There he is! After him!"

He glanced over his shoulder and saw sharks running on the tips of their fins. He wondered how they could breathe and where they had learned to hoppity-run like that. He turned back toward the elevator but tripped over a sprinkler and fell into a tuft of flowers.

"Now we've got him!" The voice sounded distant and surreal.

Shelpa gathered what remained of his senses and crawled through the grass and flowers and into the elevator. Shark fins slapped on the doors as they slid shut, and then Shelpa reached up and punched a button. The elevator rose into the sky.

He stood, rubbing his temples. Gradually, he felt better. He stared through the elevator's glass walls at stars peppering the depths of space. As the elevator rose higher, he started to get nervous. He thought he could feel the elevator twist and bend as if it were about to collapse. Or was his mind playing tricks on him? He eyed the control panel. Ten white buttons lined up in two columns, with a red one centered at the bottom and a black one at the top. One of the white ones on the right side, third from the top, was blinking.

That must be the one I pushed, he thought, and suddenly a loud, echoing clang vibrated from the floor up to his knees. A metallic rattle like loose screws clattering through the guts of a machine sounded beneath him.

His heart skipped a beat, and he panicked and pushed the red button. Immediately, a siren went off and lights flashed. A mechanism behind one of the walls whirred, and the chamber jolted to a stop. Shelpa reacted to the screaming siren and his own terror at being stationary in the middle of space by pressing the black button. The alarm stopped. The elevator now knocked and clanked, performing a series of adjustments. Then Shelpa's stomach lurched as the elevator dropped toward the surface of a strange planet, its surface littered with gray rocks and jagged boulders.

The elevator thumped down, and the doors slid open. Shelpa stepped out into ankle-deep dust. In front of him wandered creatures that resembled elephants with giraffe necks and lizard legs. Their trunks looked like trees, and their ears were attached upside down. They had hands on their heads and fingers instead of feet. He also saw insects with the heads of hippos. They hopped around on mosquito-like legs, trying to fly with wasp wings, but their heads were too heavy.

Shelpa heard a click and turned to see the elevator rising into star-speckled space. *Oh well,* he thought. *Maybe someone around here can point me in the right direction.*

He wandered up and down hills, kicking stones as he went, until he came to a crater filled with clear liquid. He looked down into the pool and saw his reflection, which seemed so real he reached out, expecting to touch flesh. His finger struck the surface and made ripples, which grew and developed into waves. The waves got larger and more turbulent, until the liquid was tossing and bubbling and shaking the ground beneath him. Shelpa backed away, slowly at first, but then quicker and quicker, as lightning clawed the sky and thunder exploded. The crater coughed flames and spit rocks.

In a kind of reluctant awe, he gazed at the sight before him.

"What in the universe is going on?" he said to himself.

CHAPTER 26

SHELPA STARED WITH eyes wide as a chariot appeared, riding on a tongue of fire and pulled by tornadoes that scattered sand and stardust. Reins extended from the tornadoes into a sphere of light. As the chariot approached, Shelpa could see that a bright, glowing being was driving, with the reins gripped in its left hand and a whip in its right. A crown covered its head, and its

cape waved and flapped, snapping in the wind of its flight.

The luminous being yanked on the reins, and the chariot halted next to Shelpa. The tornadoes slowed down and then vanished. The being opened its mouth to speak, but its nose, which seemed to have a will of its own, came loose and darted up its forehead. The eyes reacted as if this had happened before, and tried to block the nose, but they were too late. The nose slipped between them, and the eyes bumped into each other. Soon every part of the face was scrambling around, trying to seize the nose, until finally an eyebrow grabbed hold of one nostril long enough for an ear to get a grip on the other one. As the nose snorted and sneezed, trying to free itself, the lips lined up and, working with the tongue, explained to the nose that the face could not function unless it, the nose, stayed still and played its part. Eventually, with a sniff of understanding, the nose surrendered, and the face re-formed.

Shelpa wet his lips. His skin tingled, and he found standing still difficult. He stepped forward. "Are you the light spirit?"

The being nodded, beams of light radiating from its eyes like solar flares.

"I was told you could help me. I'm looking for someone. Do you know where to find her?"

Staring into its brightness, Shelpa understood the spirit was speaking, but its words were without sound.

"Your question can be answered," the spirit said, "but only by you. All things, including myself, are pieces of a grand puzzle, and we each have our own part to play."

Shelpa bit his lip. "I'm sorry. I don't understand."

The spirit aimed a twinkling finger at Shelpa's chest, and Shelpa felt a hand take hold of his heart. "Your misfortune is what happened to your sister. She has left a hole in your soul. You must make peace with your pain."

Shelpa winced as if a bandage had been ripped off his arm. "I can do that. I want to do that."

The spirit smiled. "Then you're halfway to being healed." The spirit clapped its hands above its head, and lightning flashed through the air, forming a bubble of electricity that floated, sparking and swirling, in front of Shelpa's face. The bubble popped, leaving a bright, white key, which Shelpa plucked from the air. The key was radiant, but it was also wet and sticky like whipped cream. Written along its shaft were the words SECOND KEY. Charged with excitement, Shelpa unzipped his chest pocket and put the whipped-cream key next to the cookie key. As soon as he zipped the pocket closed, lightning zapped his chest, shooting voltage through his arms and legs until he jerked straight and stiff and every hair on his body stood on end.

Shelpa suddenly found himself in the barrel again, floating downstream. He saw signs that read CAUTION! and RAPIDS! The last one read DEAD END!

Shelpa and the barrel passed the last sign and shot ahead like a torpedo. He searched frantically for a lever, button, or other device to stop the speeding barrel. At his foot, he found a pedal. He gulped and took a breath, lifted his foot, and then stamped down. The barrel stopped, and Shelpa soared head over heels through the air.

CHAPTER 27

SHELPA WAS LYING on his back with his limbs sprawled. His head was spinning, and the Xyzyx was shining hot on his face. He opened his eyes, but the shock of light slammed them shut again. So he covered his eyes with both hands and then inched his fingers apart in order to adjust bit by bit to the brightness.

"It's about time you woke up. I was starting to worry."

Shelpa sat up, rubbing his head, and found Smiley perched on a stump.

"It's you! How? When?"

"Believe it or not, a little bird told me."

"A bird?"

"Exactly. After I left the cottage, I barged through a grove of pepper trees, and I started sneezing. That gave me second thoughts. After all, we've both got to get back to the beach, right? Better if we stick together."

"How did sneezing make you think that?"

Smiley rolled her eyes. "Remember what I said about harmonizing your vibrations? If I'd been calm and relaxed, the pepper trees would have left me alone. But I was irritated from arguing with you, and the trees sensed my frustration, got nervous themselves, and peppered me." Smiley leaned forward on her stem and rested her blossom on her leaves. "From now on, you can be as bossy as you like, but don't expect me to obey you unless I want to."

"Okay, but the bird?"

"After I stopped sneezing, I wanted to go back to the cottage, but of course I couldn't. There's no turning back in this funny forest, right? But then one of the birds from the beach came whistling over my blossom, flapping its wings and chirping like crazy. I had a hunch the bird wanted me to follow, and it led me here. Sure enough, after a peaceful nap and a short wait, you came swishing through the air and landed right there. How's your arm? The way it was angled, I thought it might be broken."

Shelpa bent his elbow and rubbed his arm. "No, I'm okay, I think. My shoulder hurts a little, though."

"Let's get going. If those birds are around here, maybe the beach is nearby, too."

Shelpa stood up and sniffed the air. He noticed a

mossy smell mixed with jasmine. The trail they followed was choked with weeds and tangled vegetation, but it was also freckled with blossoming flowers that made Smiley ooh and aah.

"Do you feel any connection to flowers like these?" Shelpa asked. "I mean, they don't walk or talk, like you do."

"Pixians feel connected to all things. It's like we're part of a chain, where every link connects to every other link. That's part of the Law of Loops. So, yes, I feel linked to these flowers, and also to the trees, the grass, the sky, the wind, everything. We're all part of the same life force."

"Really? You feel just as connected to weeds as you do to flowers?"

"Is your heart more important than your head?"

"No, I guess not."

"If your right hand slaps your left hand, who feels the pain?"

"I do, of course."

"Exactly. They're all part of the same life force, which is you, and you're part of a larger life force, which includes everything you can see and imagine."

"That's discouraging."

"Discouraging? Why?"

"Look at the Xyzyx. I'd hate to think I'm part of *that* thing."

Smiley stopped in her tracks and gazed up at the sky. "Are you kidding? It's extraordinary."

He aimed a shining finger skyward. "You call that extraordinary? It's sickly. It looks like it's about to barf all over us."

"Really? Is that what you see?"

Shelpa looked up. At first he saw the same puffy-eyed star he had seen before, weak and unwell, but then he noticed that the Xyzyx looked better. The circles under its eyes were lighter. Its nose was less red and not at all runny. "On second thought, it seems to be on the road to recovery."

"You know, Shelpa, the fact that you see the Xyzyx differently than I do must mean something. I see a heavenly, dazzling, magnificent star. I wonder if the Xyzyx mirrors our vibrations. Or maybe the Xyzyx reflects something inside you, like a bad feeling or a painful memory."

Shelpa shivered. He felt a tightening in his chest. "That's possible," he said, whispering the words.

"Let's try an experiment. Think positively. Try to see the Xyzyx as perfect, healthy, happy, and whole."

Shelpa closed his eyes and concentrated. In his mind's eye, he imagined the Xyzyx as Smiley had described it. Once he had an image of the Xyzyx he hoped to see, he opened his eyes and looked at the sky. He shook his head. "No, it's still the same."

"Oh well, it was worth a try, right?"

But then again, Shelpa thought, *the dark circles seem to be disappearing, and more color is glowing in its lips.*

Soon stalks of purplish grass bordered the trail, and boulders shaped like mushrooms dotted the landscape. Shelpa's footsteps crunched leaves and snapped twigs, while Smiley's steps were as quiet as the light shining on the land.

Shelpa stared down at his feet as he walked. "Listen, I'm really sorry."

"For what?"

"Being bossy and mean. For yelling. Everything."

Smiley waved a leaf in the air. "That's okay. I forgive you. And I'm sorry, too."

"*You're* sorry? For what?"

"It's my fault we're lost in the forest, right? You only came because you were looking for me."

Shelpa licked his lips and heaved a sigh. "Actually, no, I mean, I've realized—" He cut short what he was about to say, and pointed up the path. "Look!" This time, the kangaroo was waiting for him. It pointed its tail at Shelpa and then angled the tail so the tip pointed at the sky. Both Shelpa and Smiley gazed up at puffs of clouds like flocks of gargantuan sheep crossing the sky. When Shelpa looked back down, the kangaroo was gone, and he saw a word written with darker grains of sand on the path: APOLOGETIC. Shelpa blushed. He felt warmth radiating throughout his body and wondered if he could be shining on the inside.

Smiley was the first to speak. "Yep. I see it, too."

"You know, every time I see these words, I feel better about myself, more confident."

"That's wonderful!"

"What's wonderful?"

"Don't you get it? Seeing these words is helping you."

"I agree, but how?"

"Who knows and who cares? The important thing is that they're boosting your self-esteem."

"But why would the kangaroo keep pointing at me and then pointing upward? It doesn't make sense."

"I'm not sure, but I'm thinking about it."

The trail dipped to the right and then curved back around a cluster of trees. As Shelpa walked by the trees, their branches reached forward and tickled him with twigs and leaves. Though he fought them off, knocking away the branches and slapping at the leaves, he laughed and chuckled.

"See that?" Smiley said. "Even the forest senses your better vibrations!"

Shelpa continued to laugh long after they had left the tickling trees behind, and he was still giggling when the trail opened onto a breezy meadow. He could see that the shadows of the trees around them were growing longer.

Smiley tapped Shelpa's shoulder. "Looky here." She indicated a signpost in the middle of the meadow. They walked over to it and found a map, roughly sketched but easy enough to understand. Most of the map consisted of triangles representing vegetation, but Shelpa saw a spiky shape marked Mt. Timber, an oval in the middle identified as Balooga Lake, and an area at the top right corner labeled Sandy Beach.

"Quite a way to go still," Shelpa said, adding, "at least we're heading in the right direction. That's encouraging."

Smiley pointed to the oval. "If we can get across this lake, we'll save a ton of time."

"True. Otherwise we'll have to walk all the way around it. That would take too long."

Smiley shied away from a slug that was slithering through a clump of stringy weeds near her roots, and said, "And there won't be any of these creepy crawlies."

"Don't be silly. You're bothered by bugs and stuff?" Shelpa asked her, remembering her reaction to the grasshoppers.

They heard a rustling sound and glanced at the ground near a pile of leaves. A tarantula as fat and hairy as an ape's hand crawled past them and into a cluster of bushes.

"Yes," she said, "I am."

CHAPTER 28

SOON THEY WERE descending a tree-fringed path toward the lake. Shelpa heard lapping water and smelled algae in the air. Snail-like creatures with blue shells dotted the trees, making the leaves they clung to droop and leaving silvery lines along the branches. The lake appeared and disappeared from view as the trail twisted and turned around snarled vines and grassy vegetation. The way straightened out at last, and Shelpa and Smiley stepped onto the muddy banks of Balooga Lake.

The sky overhead was bumpy with red clouds. Wind rippled the lake's surface, sending miniature waves splattering on the shore. They had hiked only a short way along the water's edge when they saw a dock. Turning toward it, they found a boat tied to a post. The boat rocked back and forth as Smiley climbed in, and then Shelpa untied the rope, jumped in, and shoved off. He picked up a paddle and started paddling. They watched a group of geese float by. The leader seemed to be the mother, and the others, smaller and whiter, trailed in line behind her. With a whisk of the paddle over the water, Shelpa splashed the last one, and it hurried ahead and bumped into another gosling.

Shelpa set down the paddle and leaned his back against the edge of the boat. As they floated freely, waves slapped against the boat's hull. Shelpa let his arm hang over the side of the boat and skimmed the water with his fingertips. He frowned and, after tugging at the skin on his throat, took a deep breath. "You asked earlier if I'd ever seen a blue kangaroo. Well, I had a little sister named Maya. She had a blue kangaroo. It was her favorite toy."

Smiley's eyes moved from the shadow of a cloud on the water to Shelpa's shining eyes.

"I've never been able to talk about this, not with anyone, but . . . I feel like I should now, or that I have to." Shelpa pressed his knees together. He stared at the water.

Smiley sat silent, her stem straight, her blossom tilted to the side.

"I was at a lake with my parents. Not exactly a lake, actually. On Shine, we have oil spills. It's hard to explain, but anyway, the lakes are not as nice as this. We were on vacation, and my parents asked me to keep an eye on Maya." He pushed his thumbs into his temples. "Gosh, this is hard."

"How old was she?" Smiley's voice was soft and gentle.

Shelpa's eyes grew watery, and he bit down on his trembling lip. "Three. She was three years old."

"Go on."

"My parents were knee-deep in the inky water, playing squareball. Maya was about ten feet away from me, up to her waist in an oil slick. She was smacking the oil with a plastic shovel, and I was watching her, but I was watching my parents, too. My mom kept glancing at Maya and me, making sure we were there. Once she even missed the ball because she was looking our way, and my dad growled at her because they were up to 121 hits. Their record was 157. For him, a trip wasn't a trip

THE SHINING ADVENTURES OF SHELPA MCSTORM

unless they broke their record.

"At one point, they got a rally going, and you could hear the excitement in my dad's voice even while he was warning my mom to stay calm. He started hitting the ball with more calculated strokes while counting out loud: '144, 145, 146.' His voice got louder and louder: '151, 152!' My mom was concentrating like crazy. She didn't want to be the one who blew it.

"By 157, my dad was practically shouting the numbers: '158, 159!' But then my mom missed the ball. Actually, she let it fly past her without even trying to hit it. She was facing me, and at first I thought she was looking at me, but she was looking *through* me. Her head started swiveling, and her eyes were sweeping up and down the shore. That's when I realized Maya was missing, and all the air whooshed out of my lungs as if someone had socked me in the stomach. My eyes went wide open and I looked around too, figuring she had to be there, sitting on the asphalt or scratching a hole in some tar somewhere."

Shelpa's shine dimmed. "My dad understood immediately. He dropped the stick and started rushing back and forth, shouting her name, but the beach was packed with people. I mean, she could have been right there, and we might not have seen her. There were that many people. I started calling her name, too, and noticed that my mom had headed one way up the shore, and my dad was searching the area where our beach chairs were, so I figured I'd go the other way from my mom.

"I kept thinking I'd find her, or that somebody would, and then everything would be okay. I'd be embarrassed and I'd probably get in trouble, but that would be nothing compared to having Maya back. I promised myself I'd never let her out of my sight again. Not ever."

Smiley's voice came as quiet as a mouse's squeak. "Oh my."

And for the first time since Shelpa had met her, Smiley frowned, tears appearing in the corners of her eyes.

CHAPTER 29

SHELPA CONSIDERED STOPPING when he noticed Smiley's tears, but she signaled with a leaf, urging him to finish what he had started. So he continued, "The farther down the shore I went, the more worried I became. I kept looking at different parts of the spill, expecting to see Maya's body floating facedown. Then I checked the area around the grease pools and tar pits, searching for someone running off with Maya tucked under an arm. Shine's a dangerous place. People are crazy. It wouldn't have been strange if she'd been kidnapped.

"I'd gone pretty far down the beach by then. About ten minutes had passed, and I was really scared. My heart was somersaulting. I kept looking back over my shoulder, hoping to see someone waving at me to come back, shouting that they'd found her."

Smiley stared unblinking at Shelpa's face. Her leaves were covering her mouth.

Shelpa rubbed his hands together as if he were washing them. "You know in a dream when you're sure what's happening is happening, but really it's not? Everything's blurry, but still you're convinced it's real? That's what it was like when I saw her." Tears welled up in his eyes, and his voice cracked as he continued. "I was making my way back to our place on the beach, still eyeballing every square inch of the oil spill, the slicks, the asphalt, everywhere, when I saw someone dragging her out of a tar pit."

Shelpa pulled up a pocket and used it to wipe his eyes. "The next thing I remember was my parents pushing through the crowd and finding me in the middle. When they saw Maya's body on the ground next to me—covered with black goop—that was the end of everything."

"What did they do? I mean, I can't even imagine."

"My mom screamed, and then she slumped to the ground as if the bones in her body had gone soft. My father started shoving people, yelling at them to stop staring and to run for help. But a doctor was already there. She'd done all she could do." The corners of Shelpa's mouth were locked in a frown. He slumped forward with his arms at his sides, his legs straight out.

"I'm sorry if this makes you sad, but I thought you should know. My parents haven't trusted me since then. Not until this morning, when they left us alone on the beach. That was why I couldn't let you leave. That's why I followed you into the forest."

"Oh, Shelpa! If I'd had any idea."

"It's not your fault. I'm not blaming you. I've got to stop blaming other people for my own problems. Everything that happens to me is my fault."

"Don't think like that. Your sister's death isn't your fault. After all, your parents were there, too. They were watching her also."

"Yeah, but I was in charge. They'd trusted me to keep an eye on her, and I failed. Not a day goes by that I don't think about her. Maya's the first thing on my mind every morning, and my last thought before bed. I've replayed that afternoon in my head a million times, imagining all kinds of situations in which she was saved. I dream she's alive sometimes, and it's wonderful while it lasts, but when I wake up, it's like someone flipped a switch and illuminated a hole so deep that nothing could ever fill it. I wish I had the words to describe what it feels like. Empty, hollow, lost . . . None of those words, or even all of them together, is enough."

Shelpa shifted to take the weight off his spine, which had been resting on the hard edge of the boat's wooden frame. "Sometimes when I watch people and I see how easily they laugh or smile, I wish I could be like them. I mean people whose laughs and smiles start in the pit of their stomachs and then beam out, not only through their mouths but from their eyes and ears, too. When I see those smiles and hear those laughs, I know that those people don't have a hole like I have. They don't have parents who worry about putting too much responsibility on their shoulders because they think they can't handle it. I feel that every day, and I watch what I say and do. I worry, and my parents worry about me worrying, and that makes me feel like it's my job to show them they don't have to worry. So when my dad asked me to keep an eye on you, you have to understand what he was trying to do. He was giving me a second chance. Finally."

Smiley was weeping quietly, wiping tears from her eyes. "I don't know what to say. I'm really sorry."

Shelpa closed his eyes, shaking his head and thinking about Maya. As the boat bobbed over some swells, he opened his eyes again and saw Smiley's leaves pressed flat against the floor.

"You'd better start paddling again," she said. "Otherwise we'll never get across this lake. And don't worry about me. I won't run off again. We'll get through this together. I promise."

"What makes you so sure?"

"For one thing, they certainly know we're missing by now. There must be a search party or rescuers or somebody looking for us, and we might even manage to get back to the beach before they find us. We made it this far on our own, right? Hey, I know! Let's light a fire. Then they'll be able to find us easier."

Shelpa shivered, remembering the fire he had thought was going to kill him on Mount Timber. What he said, though, was, "But then we'd have to stay in one place, and wait, and if they don't see it . . . Besides, you'll wilt, and it'll be dark in a few hours. I say we try to get back on our own."

And the last thing we need is another fire, he thought. *We're likely to burn down the whole forest.*

CHAPTER 30

SHELPA PADDLED, and kept paddling even when the muscles in his arms got sore and his back started to ache. The air was breezy, and trees lined the distant banks. Clothed with yellow, orange, and violet vegetation, the forest swept up and over the surrounding hills. With the red sky and blue-green water, Shelpa imagined he was going through a rainbow.

Smiley pushed herself up, leaned over the boat's side, and splashed water on her blossom.

While he paddled, Shelpa watched a bird swoop down toward a small island that held a single bush rising like a shock of green smoke. The bird disappeared into the tangle of twigs and leaves and reemerged with a stick bug dangling from its beak. The bird snapped its head back, swallowed the bug whole, and then flew off, squawking and beating its wings.

Smiley's stomach growled. "I'm so hungry I could eat just about anything right now."

"Could you eat a dragonfly's eye smothered with tree sap?"

"Gross!"

"I didn't think so."

They were silent for a few seconds, and then Smiley asked, "What would happen if you couldn't shine?"

"Actually, there was one kid once. He couldn't shine."

"Why not? Couldn't someone teach him?"

"Shining isn't something you learn. It's something you do, like breathing or thinking."

"So what happened to him?"

"One day, some neighborhood kids followed him home from school. As he was walking through an alley, they surrounded him, backed him into a corner, and insisted he shine."

"That's awful! What a bully you are!"

"I wasn't there! I heard this story at school the next day."

Smiley stared at Shelpa with her blossom tilted and one eye closed.

"Really! I had nothing to do with it. I'm just answering your question."

"Okay, go ahead."

"He couldn't shine, but he certainly tried. He

jumped up and down on one leg while quacking like a duck. He squatted on his heels and strutted around like a chicken looking for a place to lay an egg. Nothing worked. Finally, his face turned serious, his lower lip bulged, he held his breath, and with his hands and teeth clenched, he tried to shine by sheer force of will."

"So what happened?"

"He farted."

"Ick!"

"But that's what did it! Everyone started laughing like lunatics, including the kid, and the thing is, while he was laughing, he started shining. Not too bright, but with enough of a glow to prove he had it in him. From then on they called him Dim, because he shined but not a lot."

Smiley slapped her leaves together and smiled. "That goes to show that you should never give up."

"Exactly," Shelpa said. "Always believe in yourself."

The boat slipped through the water as Shelpa spotted an outlet and paddled into it. Traveling through a stream now, they saw grass and waterweeds fringing the banks on both sides, growing above and below the water. Ahead, a strip of vegetation divided the stream into two routes. To Shelpa, the one on the left looked like the obvious choice. Unobstructed, the water flowed smoothly, while in the other route, jutting rocks and knotted sticks cluttered the surface. He could see branches with splintered ends breaking the surface and, further off, white-water rapids.

"Left?" Shelpa asked.

Smiley lifted her blossom, inspected both ways, and said, "Right." Then she lay back down.

Shelpa's lips quivered as he second-guessed himself. He decided to trust Smiley's judgment and, shrugging his shoulders, steered to the right. The boat became more difficult to control as the current increased, and Shelpa panicked, paddling in circles as they scraped over a lump of weeds, grazed against branches, and then entered the rapids sideways.

Smiley was sitting up now, alarmed.

"What's going on?"

Shelpa rubbed his chin. "You said 'right.'"

"Of course I said 'right.' You said 'left,' and I agreed with you!"

Shelpa wanted to smack himself. "Well, it's too late now. Hold on!"

Smiley clung to the boat's frame as Shelpa dumped the paddle inside the boat and wrapped his arms around her. They struggled to hold on as water spilled inside and soaked them. The boat reeled and tipped, grated against an overgrown root, and then banged into a rock. Smiley almost fell out, but Shelpa held her tight.

The boat bumped against one last boulder, and then the current slackened and the river emptied into a pool. Shelpa released Smiley, grabbed the paddle, and paddled along quietly. He looked at her with an apologetic expression, but Smiley just smiled. "That was fun!"

Soon they were floating past trees with hanging limbs and tattered branches that cast shadows on the water. The trees' roots protruded like tentacles from the bank. Shelpa steered toward the right bank, angling into a clump of roots. They jerked forward as the boat's bottom scraped over sand. Shelpa climbed out of the boat, offered Smiley his hand, and helped her onto shore.

Biting his lip, he gazed up at the Xyzyx, which looked healthier now. No longer sneezing or coughing, it was smiling radiantly. Half sun, half moon, the Xyzyx shone with a zigzag line blazed down its center, dividing sunlight from moonlight. The two halves appeared to be separate, and yet they were part of the same star. He marveled at the idea of two forces, such different energies, operating as a single entity. But how much longer would its light last? The sun side was yawning, and the moon part was twitching in a dream.

CHAPTER 31

SHELPA AND SMILEY left the boat and started walking. According to the map they had seen, Sandy Beach was ahead of them. They walked along the stream's bank, hoping it would lead them to the ocean. From there, they could find their way back to Big Toe Hotel by going along the beach.

After an hour, Smiley was dragging her roots. "How about a short break? Five minutes?"

Shelpa did not want to stop, but he thought about how tired Smiley must be. Wiping the sweat from his face, he quietly agreed.

Just then, he noticed loose strands of reeds floating downstream, forming the word SYMPATHETIC.

"There's another one," he told Smiley.

Smiley looked where Shelpa was pointing.

"The kangaroo?"

"What else?"

They sat under the branches of a slouching tree on patches of soft, gray grass. Smiley sketched shapes in the sand with the tip of a leaf. She was drawing a happy face when Shelpa said, "By the way, I've got another key." He unzipped his pocket and pulled out the whipped-cream key.

Smiley took the key in her leaf. She blinked against its flickering radiance as she inspected it closely. Then she handed it back. "Odd."

"Any ideas?" Shelpa asked.

"Maybe the words are like tests for you to earn the keys."

"But I got the cookie key after I'd seen four words. This one came after only three words: 'practical,' 'level-headed,' and 'honest.'"

"Perhaps it gets easier as you go along."

A petal drooped over Smiley's eyes. She brushed back the petal and drew a heart in the sand. "Maybe the keys mean that you've reached a higher level of self-awareness. Keys open doors, of course, so they might symbolize some sort of tranquility or insight you're being opened up to."

For a minute, they were quiet, and Shelpa heard the hum of insects and croaking frogs.

Then Smiley said, "I was thinking, maybe the kangaroo wasn't pointing at the trees or the clouds. Maybe it was pointing at the Xyzyx. You said the Xyzyx looked awful, but then it was a bit better."

"A lot better, actually."

"So maybe the kangaroo was trying to explain that there's a connection between you and the Xyzyx, and when you see the Xyzyx healing, it means you're healing, too."

Shelpa sat up straighter. "You mean Maya? My parents? That whole thing?"

Smiley stared at Shelpa, her face as still as a portrait. "Do you have any better ideas?"

CHAPTER 32

SHELPA AND SMILEY set off again. After they had walked steadily for a while, Shelpa sensed salt in the air, so he suggested they leave the stream in order to climb to the top of a hill. When they got to the top and saw the ocean, they high-fived each other.

"All right!" Shelpa exclaimed. "We're home free. We just head to the water now and then follow the coast back to Sandy Beach."

At the beach, they found tomatoes swinging on swing sets and celery sticks sliding down slides—a scene only their growling stomachs could explain. Coconut trees lined the coast, stretching into the distance toward a crouton as high as a hill. Halfway between the slides and the crouton, Shelpa saw a tree with lemon-colored leaves that was rooted in the middle of a pumpkin patch.

They walked toward the tree, and as they neared,

Shelpa saw avocados hanging from its branches. The tree was strumming a guitar with the twigs of a branch, and the avocados snapped back and forth as the tree twisted and jerked. At the twang of the last string, the tree bowed and the pumpkins applauded, some knocking against each other and shouting, "Encore!"

The tree leafed a few chords and then said, "Pumpkins, you playful little pilgrims you, I had a freaky dream last night."

"Hurray! It's dream-telling time!" The pumpkins rolled around in a frenzy, some shouting, "Who's first?" while others yelled, "Me!"

"Hrrrmph!" The tree indicated itself with the tip of a twig. "I'll go first, of course. I brought it up, after all."

The pumpkins pushed forward, scrambling to move closer to the tree's trunk. When the tree set the guitar down on a patch of grass, two pumpkins fought to hold it. They tugged back and forth and side to side, yanking and arguing until the tree intervened.

"You can hold it," the tree said to one of the pumpkins. "And you can admire it," the tree said to the other.

The pumpkins decided to take turns holding and admiring the guitar, and also promised not to pluck the strings.

Then the tree began. "I was lonesome, neither fruits nor vegetables nearby. I longed for friends, someone to sing to, but I was all alone."

Some pumpkins moaned and others sobbed, but then the tree stiffened and said, "Suddenly, a speck appeared on the horizon. I thought it was a bird at first, coming to build its nest in my branches. How overly optimistic and naive! As the speck neared, becoming bigger and fatter and foul, what I saw made me shake from the tips of my leaves to the ends of my roots." The tree paused and made eye contact with each pumpkin before continuing. "It was a lumberjack, with biceps stretching out his shirtsleeves to twice their size. He had crooked yellow teeth and a stare that could have carved initials in stone. He had an ax slung over his shoulder."

The pumpkins were so silent that Shelpa thought he could hear his heart beating.

"The lumberjack stopped in front of me. He hacked into my trunk, swinging the ax as if attacking an enemy, blow after blow, until finally I toppled over and fell to the ground. Then, leaving my leaves and roots to rot, he chopped me into pieces. He did the same to three other trees, and though we screamed in agony and begged for mercy, he ignored us as if we were just silent blocks of wood."

Pumpkins glanced around with wide-eyed expressions and frowning mouths.

"What bothers me most," the tree said, "is that he used me to build a house, and though I was filled with the love of his family inside, I still felt empty, with a void in my soul as wide as the sky. Drenched with dew, I woke to the sound of a willow weeping." Looking around with questions in his eyes, the tree asked, "Well? Any interpretations?"

"It's obvious, isn't it?" one pumpkin blurted out.

"It means you're going to die."

The tree's leaves trembled, and its anxious expression melted into a scowl. Another pumpkin saved the day, shouting, "Perhaps you need a wife! Maybe you should marry!"

The tree chuckled, instantly cheered. "Me? Marry? Why, that's preposterous!"

Shelpa raised a hand. "Could I ask a question?"

Every pumpkin in the patch turned toward Shelpa, and the tree frowned. But were they waiting for him to speak . . . or for the right moment to attack?

CHAPTER 33

UNNERVED AT BEING the sudden focus of attention, Shelpa scratched his neck and smiled awkwardly. Smiley elbowed him. He glanced at her, then turned back to the staring pumpkins and expectant tree. "My friend and I are looking for Sandy Beach," he said. "If you could just point us—"

The sound of shuddering leaves interrupted him. A humongous meatball with bloodshot eyes, two muscular arms, and saliva dribbling from the corners of its mouth rolled right up to Shelpa.

"Bkflm xjr ipt?" it growled.

Shelpa stuck a hand in his pocket and felt for the saw, but then he remembered losing it in the whirlpool. Grinning awkwardly, he looked around for help, but the tree was as still as a lamppost, and the pumpkins were mute. Smiley stood as stiff as a board.

"I'm s-s-sorry," Shelpa finally said. "I d-don't understand."

Sauce seethed from the meatball's pores as it roared, "BKFLM XJR IPT!"

Afraid to offend the raving meatball, Shelpa did not respond. He worried that the wrong word could lead to chaos, confusion, and shredded beef.

The meatball rolled closer, its eyes crossed, and snarled, "Fekfo juq QICCR ooxfiox? Erneki jei aowpqm TEHDF!"

Sweat beaded Shelpa's brow, and he tucked his lower lip behind his teeth. The meatball reached forward as if to tear Shelpa to pieces just as Shelpa saw an apple, a short distance away, with a bow aimed in their direction. He heard the sound of a pop, and a ripe plum hurtled through the air. The meatball rolled off in a hurry. Shelpa ducked, but not in time, and the plum splattered against his face, covering him with pulp.

Blinded by plum juice, he heard a gruff voice shout, "Seize him!"

Pumpkins tittered and a guitar string snapped as Shelpa was grabbed by his shirtsleeves and dragged to the ground. When his sight cleared, he saw a corps of apples surrounding him. He saw several other apples holding Smiley by the leaves.

One of the apples, a red one, said, "You have been

captured and are a prisoner of the Apple Corps. Surrender at once!"

Four apple-core badges lined its chest, and Shelpa stared at it until one of the three-core apples turned and said, "He doesn't have to surrender. We've already captured him!"

Four-core turned to Three-core and hollered, "The rules say he has to!"

"They do not!" Three-core shouted. "They don't say anything like that!"

"Yes, they do!" Four-core howled, bumping Three-core with its belly and knocking it to the ground. "Prisoners have to surrender no matter what! The rules insist, and besides, I say so!"

Three-core rose to its feet, wiped dirt off its uniform,

and mumbled under its breath, "No, they don't."

Four-core grinned with a mouth that seemed to stretch all the way around its head. Then it turned to an apple with no cores. "Pip! Proclaim the penalty for surrenders!"

The apple stumbled forward, unrolled a scroll, and read in a rehearsed voice: "'Anyone who surrenders after being captured by the Apple Corps will serve three seasons in a cherry pit.'" Pip then rolled up the scroll and returned to formation.

Shelpa lifted his chin. "Then I don't surrender."

Four-core's two apple-seed eyes sprouted. "But you *have* to surrender. Those are the rules of Apple Corps."

"But I'm not playing Apple Corps."

"Did he just say what he said?" asked a two-core.

"He thinks he's not playing?" asked a one-core.

"It's not up to you," Four-core explained. "You have to play, whether you want to or not. That's the *other* rule."

Shelpa tucked his hands under his armpits. "I refuse to surrender."

Four-core gazed at the ground, puzzled. "This has never happened before. We'll have to put you in the pit until the judge decides what to do with you." And with that, Shelpa was clubbed on the head and remembered no more.

CHAPTER 34

SHELPA'S HEAD WAS throbbing when he regained consciousness. His shine was a mere spark, and his surroundings were as black as night.

"Smiley," he said, his voice echoing, "are you here?"

No answer came, and he sighed, hoping she was safe.

He was lying flat on his back in a puddle of what felt like mud but smelled mostly like cherries. He was hungry, so he raised a hand to his face and licked his finger. Instantly he retched, choked, and spit. The substance tasted like rotten eggs and something else that suggested a foulness he did not want to think about.

As he started to get up, he heard a slurping sound. Someone or something was squishing through the mire toward him. With twisted nerves and dread knotting his guts, he backed away and felt for a wall or weapon. Before he could find anything, he sensed a presence in front of him, its breath heating his forehead. Shelpa froze, gripped by terror, and started shivering all over.

"Achooo!" Someone sneezed in his face.

No longer afraid but furious, Shelpa wiped his eyes, nose, and mouth. "That's disgusting!"

"Thorry," a nasal, hissing voice responded. "I'm thick. It thort of thnuck out when I wasn't exthpecting it. My name'th Thkinnybone Joneth. Nithe to meet you."

Shelpa reached out, searching for a hand to shake. Finding nothing, he said, "I'm sorry. I can't see. It's too dark."

"Courthe, it'th dark. We're in a pit. You can put your hand down."

"Wait a minute . . . you can see?"

"It taketh time, but your eyeth adjutht."

"How long have you been here?"

"For ath long ath I can remember."

"That's terrible! What did you do wrong?"

"You mean, what did I do *right?* Being here'th an honor. I'm the keeper of the third key."

"Really?" Shelpa started to shimmer, but the dank air depressed him, and his shine flickered out.

"Where is it?"

"It'th here, but to get it, you firtht have to eat thome of thith pit."

"Are you kidding me? I already have! It's horrible!"

"That'th becauthe you ate from over there. That'th where I uh, well, anyway, try thome from thith thide. Here, hold out your hand."

Shelpa felt something plop onto his palm. He cringed but then held the goop to his nose, sniffed, and smelled cherry. Poking his tongue out as far as possible, he tasted the substance. The flavor was sweet and tangy. He tried some more, and suddenly his attention turned inward as visions flitted in and out of his mind like hummingbirds. All at once, as if a nest of understanding had been built in his head, he knew what he had to do to harmonize his vibrations and make peace with his parents and with himself. In his mind's eye, he could see himself hiking to a spot right there in the forest, not far from where he was. He knew he had to go there, though why or what was waiting for him was unclear. He understood only that his salvation depended on that place.

CHAPTER 35

SHELPA WAS SO EXCITED that he filled the pit with light. Then he saw Skinnybone Jones coiled up and cowering in a corner.

"You're a snake!" Shelpa shouted. He pointed a finger as if accusing the reptile of having deceived him.

"What did you ethpect?" Skinnybone asked. "An orangutan, an aardvark, a duck-billed platyputh?"

"No, I guess not. But . . . hey! What's that around your neck?"

"That, my friend, ith your third and final key." The snake glided forward and stopped an arm's length away from Shelpa. "The keyth are nethethary to open the phythical doorth you'll find. But the pit was nethethary to open the mental doorth in your mind. After all, now everything'th clear, right? And you know where to go."

Shelpa nodded. Carefully, he lifted the key—smooth,

shiny, and as red as a cherry—off the snake's neck. He read its shaft: THIRD KEY. Elated, he dropped the key into his pocket, next to the other keys. He wondered again where Smiley was. He was about to ask Skinnybone if he knew anything when he heard a latch unhook high above. A crack of light appeared. Looking up, he saw the raw ceiling and an open trapdoor. Several shadows entered the pit, dropping down on ropes.

"Uh-oh," Skinnybone said, slinking away as apples splashed into the slime.

The apples seized Shelpa, tying his wrists behind his back, and then one of them shouted, "Okay, Pip! Haul him up!"

Once he was out of the pit, Shelpa saw light shining through the branches of trees, and apples armed with toothpicks. But then a blindfold was wrapped around his eyes, and a toothpick jabbed the back of his heel. He jumped at the unexpected prick.

He marched forward and got jabbed with toothpicks whenever he slowed down. Though the air was chilly, the rapid pace kept him warm, and he wondered how the apples, with their puny legs and short stride, managed to keep up. He listened to the rhythmic crunching of their feet, marching over a trail laden with dry leaves, and imagined their life of drills, orders, and mindless monotony. Then he banged his head on a branch, and the apples laughed as if they had steered him into the branch on purpose. With his hands tied, he could not reach up to protect himself or rub away the pain.

Several stabs in the shin told Shelpa to stop. He was then pushed across a threshold, and his wrists were unbound. He sensed the heat of attention and heard a murmur of voices as he was shoved along and then forced to sit. Someone removed his blindfold, and when his sight adjusted to the light, he saw he was sitting on a stump in a garden, surrounded by string beans, turnips, broccoli, papayas, and a radish.

Smiley was there, too, sitting between an artichoke and an eggplant. She waved a leaf, and Shelpa waved back in great relief. Then a cucumber stepped into the center of the clearing and announced, "All rise! Judge Jalapeño presiding."

At that, a jalapeño pepper appeared between two bushes and, in a spicy tone, said, "Enough nonsense! Let's go, Joe." After seating himself on a flat stone, he adjusted his white-haired wig, turned to Shelpa, and said, "Okay, criminal. What do you have to say for yourself?"

"Depends," Shelpa said, rubbing his chin. "What am I supposed to have done wrong?"

The judge's bloated cheeks deflated. "What do you mean? Don't you know?"

Shelpa threw his hands in the air. "I have no idea."

A vein on the judge's forehead swelled as he thumbed through a stack of papers. Finding nothing, he pushed them aside and pulled out a briefcase. After he had searched notebooks, packets, files, and folders, he spit out his breath and asked, "Dagnabbit, Joe! What's his offense?"

Joe stepped forward and recited in a monotone, "Refusing to surrender, resisting arrest, fraternizing with a meatball, assisting in a prison break, and—"

"A prison break?" the judge interrupted, pounding his gavel on the stone. "When did that happen?"

"Early this morning, sir."

The judge's skin turned a darker green. "Well? Were you planning to notify me, or were you hoping I'd read about it in the *Garden Gazette?* How many prisoners got away?"

"Thirteen pepperonis and a meatball. They've crossed Pesto State Bridge and are seeking asylum at Prince Alfredo's Pizza Palace, your honor."

"Did you say a meatball?"

"I'm sorry to say I did, sir."

"Please tell me it wasn't . . ." The judge paused and glanced up in prayer before finishing his sentence. "Maniac."

"I'm sorry to say it was, sir."

The judge's eyes sunk like rocks in the sea. He pointed a shaky finger at Shelpa. "Okay, criminal. Start talking!"

A carrot started whispering in Joe's ear, and Joe's eyes grew wider and darker. Finally, Joe stood and said, "Judge Jalapeño, sir!"

"This had better be an important interruption, Joe."

"Your honor, Maniac has been apprehended. We await your command to admit him to the current proceedings as an acquaintance of the accomplice."

"You found him? Where?"

"On Spaghetti Street, disguising himself with tomato sauce, sir."

"Well done!" the judge said, holding a fist in the air. "But do you really intend to bring him here?"

"He's tied up, Your Honor."

"Yes, of course, but . . . you know, even so."

"I assure you, sir, you'll be safe."

The judge gulped again. He scratched between his chins. "Uh, yeah, okay . . . I guess."

Soon an onion arrived, pushing a wheelbarrow with the meatball inside, hanging from a hook. Wrapped like a mummy in chains and locks, the meatball slobbered and drooled while being wheeled through the garden. The vegetables stared in horror. The judge ducked behind the flat stone he'd been sitting on and reached for his gavel.

Just then, Maniac went berserk. Emitting a bloodcurdling howl, the psycho meatball leaped off the hook, out of the wheelbarrow, and into the center of the garden, roaring, "FARFHUJENHYD! JIBIDIG DXIPTHOG! YAAAAAAAARGHHHH!"

That was as far as Maniac got. Though it struggled and spit, trying to bite through the chains and crush the locks, it could not sever its bonds. Soon reduced to a state of fury and frustration, Maniac gave up, its face mashed against the ground.

Shelpa and Smiley took this opportunity to escape, running away through the forest. After looking back several times and seeing no signs of pursuit, they slowed down and continued with caution. Fearing an ambush at every turn, they advanced with birdlike steps, peering around bushes and up into the trees.

Shelpa found the tallest tree in the area and climbed to the highest branch that would support his weight, searching for something he knew had to be close by. He saw no apples or beaches anywhere, only Mount Timber in the distance and a vast sea of treetops in every direction. Back on the ground, Shelpa stuffed his hands in his side pockets and rocked back and forth from his heels to the tips of his toes.

Smiley stood by his side. "Are we lost again?"

"Yes, though not really. I've got to do something before we try to find the beach. There's a place nearby where I have to make a quick stop."

"How do you know where to go?"

"I saw the way when I was in the cherry pit."

Smiley lifted her leaves and then dropped them by her sides. Then, together, they plodded along.

CHAPTER 36

EARLY EVENING HAD arrived. Cooler air raised goose bumps on Shelpa's skin and started Smiley's teeth chattering. They pushed past prickly shrubs and squeezed through gaps in the foliage. Shelpa's feet crunched over what looked like snow on the ground. Soon everything around them—the leaves and trunks of trees, the bushes, even the soil—gleamed white. Mist whitened the air, limiting visibility to the distance of a stone's throw. Shelpa stopped and scooped up a handful of the snowy substance. The flakes crumbled between his fingers as he touched them to his tongue and tasted sugar. The forest was covered with frosting!

They kept moving. Shelpa walked with a kick in his step, tilting his head and angling an ear. He sensed something big was about to happen. The chance to make peace with himself, and with his parents, was near. They moved forward out of the fog, and then, through a gap in the white-coated vegetation, he saw a spot of color. Shelpa was on pins and needles as they continued into a ring of trees, and what he saw in the middle of the trees made him rub his eyes and blink. He was staring up at an ice-cream cone as tall as a building, topped with three scoops: chocolate, strawberry, and highest of all, vanilla. Blood surged through his veins. He had found the place. He knew that inside that layer of vanilla, he would find the serenity he was seeking.

Shelpa turned to Smiley. He put a hand on her stem. "This is something I've got to do alone. Wait for me here. I'll be back as soon as possible."

"Okay, but hurry up. I'm c-c-cold."

Shelpa ran forward, his heart pounding with excitement. Ahead of him he saw the cone planted in the ground. Reaching the cone, he found a lever on its side. He lifted the lever, and a door-sized section of the cone retracted and slid to the side. Stepping inside, he found steps that continued upward, ending at an escalator that circled the inside of the cone to the first scoop.

Around and around he went, as if he were climbing the interior of a metal spring. At the top of the escalator stood a door that looked and smelled like a cookie. He unzipped his pocket and pulled out the first key. He held his breath, biting his lower lip and praying the key would not crumble in the keyhole. He figured that if worse came to worst he could eat his way through, but luckily the key turned, and Shelpa heard hinges crunch as the door scraped forward. Cookie crumbs and chocolate chips rained over his head and shoulders as he entered the chocolate scoop.

CHAPTER 37

SHELPA WALKED INTO a dark, eerie cavity. The floor was moist and slippery, and a low-ceilinged corridor stretched before him, disappearing into shadows and gloom. He was afraid to take a step in the darkness, but he knew he could not turn back now. He focused his thoughts on his goal of the vanilla scoop above, gathered his courage, and started groping forward. He had to feel his way through the tunnel. He wished he could shine brighter, but the dismal atmosphere prevented him.

The walls and floor were squishy and wet, and chocolate caked his feet and stained his overalls. Chocolate dripped from the ceiling into his hair, oozed down his neck, and trickled along his spine. He moved slowly, and when he tried to pick up the pace, he found the floor was slick, and he fought to stay on his feet.

As Shelpa passed a tunnel that branched off from

the main corridor, he glanced into its shadows and saw lurking in its depths an enormous reptile with green scales and black spots. Webbed wings protruded from its shoulders, and a long, forked tail rose from its lower back. The creature had a crooked horn twisting out of its head, and its eyes were full of flames. Horrified, Shelpa hurried by and passed several more tunnels that branched off from the main corridor. Voices wailed inside them, but he covered his ears and kept going, soon finding another escalator.

He rubbed a hand over his brow as he stepped onto the moving staircase. Around and around he went, spiraling upward to the strawberry scoop.

Stepping off, he found a door that looked as white and fluffy as whipped cream. He pulled the second key out of his pocket. The key slid into the keyhole and turned smoothly. He pushed open the door and stepped into the middle of a circus. He saw clowns shooting out of cannons, flying through the air, and landing in distant nets. Other clowns were running around with red ball noses and oversized boots, doing somersaults, cartwheels, and backflips. Some were driving cars the size of shoeboxes while honking horns and blowing whistles. One was upside down with his feet in the air, balancing on the tip of his pinky. Shelpa even saw clowns climbing up a ladder to a diving board high above. One clown dove into a pool of what looked like butterscotch syrup, splashing the surrounding performers.

Nearby, acrobats balanced on each other's shoulders while jugglers tossed bowling balls and watermelons with scoops of strawberry ice cream. Tightrope walkers were crossing a rope that stretched from one side of the scoop to the other. Animal trainers worked with elephants and bears, teaching them to sit up, roll over, and leap through rings of fire. Shelpa watched one trainer put his entire head into the wide-open jaws of a lion.

Shelpa started to weave his way through the confusion. He could not take a step without getting in someone's way. He had to stop, wait, and often back up and try another direction. He darted this way and that, moving as carefully as he could, and even so, he bumped into one performer after another. Acrobats complained and clowns whistled warningly. Trying to avoid one juggler, Shelpa knocked against another, who was balancing on a balloon. The juggler lost concentration and dropped a watermelon on Shelpa's head and a bowling ball on his foot. Shelpa stifled the urge to yelp as his eyes flooded with tears, and he limped on through the crowd to the next escalator.

CHAPTER 38

UP THE ESCALATOR he went, rising to his destination. His blood raced with anticipation as he stepped off the stairs—and the third key floated out of his pocket as if on wings, sailed toward a cherry-colored door, and slipped into the lock. The door evaporated in a puff of smoke, and Shelpa walked through the threshold into the vanilla ice-cream scoop, entering an atmosphere of silence and tranquility.

He plunged his hand into a soft, velvety wall and, despite the cold numbing his fingers, scooped up some ice cream. He took a bite. *Yum!*

Just then, he heard a child's giggle and the patter of footsteps. He backed away as an area of the wall blurred and a wispy form emerged. A white-skinned figure gradually took shape, stepped forward, and stood facing Shelpa. Clothed in radiant light, she had white hair that floated in tendrils around her head, and her eyes shimmered like sunlight through diamonds. She was clutching a blue kangaroo to her chest.

Shelpa stared, transfixed. He was afraid to breathe, swallow, or blink for fear she would disappear. His heart was drumming. His mouth opened and closed, but no words came.

"Hello, Shelpa." Her voice, so soft and sweet, calmed his nerves like cold water on a fresh burn.

"Is it you?" he asked, blinking back tears.

She smiled. "Yes, it's me."

"Oh, Maya! I'm so sorry. Can you ever forgive me?"

"There's no need to apologize. Only you can forgive yourself."

"But I was supposed to keep an eye on you. Your death was my fault."

"Death is nobody's fault. It's a fact of life."

"But you were so young. You were my sister."

"I'm still your sister, and you will always be my brother."

Shelpa straightened his back. "I keep wishing it hadn't happened."

"You can't undo what's already done."

"It was a mistake. I should never have taken my eyes off you."

"Life is full of mistakes. Errors are natural. You can't change the past, but you can learn from it." Maya lifted off the ground, floating several inches above the floor, and Shelpa noticed she had bright, feathery wings on her back. "Life is a journey," she continued, "and for many, it's uphill all the way. Keep climbing, and accept the suffering that balances the beauty."

"I feel so guilty."

"You gain nothing from feeling guilty. Turn my loss into your lesson."

"What can I learn from your death? How am I supposed to get over that?"

"You will never get over my death. You can only learn to see life in a new way. The key is acceptance. Concentrate on who you are now, and work hard to create the future you would like to see."

"What about you? I can't help thinking about the birthdays you'll miss, all the friends you'd have had, and the good times we'd have shared together."

"Never mind me. I am in a better place. My heaven is in your heart."

Overwhelmed with emotions, Shelpa bent forward and, covering his face with his hands, started sobbing. Grief, despair, and sorrow gripped his insides, and in his mind he saw the feelings rise through his chest and then change into the tears flowing between his fingers. He felt the knot in his chest—an ache that had taken root the moment Maya disappeared on the beach—loosen like a ball of string suddenly unraveling. The process hurt, but as the pain came to an end, he also felt cleansed, invigorated, and for the first time in a long time, free. He knew Maya was with him and always would be. Never again would they be apart.

"You have to go now," Maya told him. "You must get back to the beach."

"That's right, the beach! Can you tell me where it is? Which way should I go?"

"You are on your own, Shelpa. Everything is up to you now."

"Wait a minute! Don't go. I have so much to say, so many things to tell you!"

But Maya had already turned away. She faded more and more, until he could no longer see her.

Shelpa stood up straight, sniffed, and wiped his eyes. Then he hugged himself, imagining he was hugging Maya, too, and suddenly he felt lighter, as if he could float. Charged with the energy of a thousand shining suns, he glowed so brightly he could no longer distinguish himself from his surroundings. He wondered where he ended, where Maya began, and whether boundaries even existed.

Shelpa batted his eyes. He had to get back to Smiley, and together, they had to get back to the beach.

CHAPTER 39

SHELPA LEFT THE ICE-CREAM cone feeling exhilarated. When Smiley saw him nearly exploding with elation, she laid a leaf over her heart.

Shelpa waved his arms excitedly. "You're never going to believe what happened."

"Tell me later. First, come see this." She took Shelpa's hand and led him along a path that curved around a short tree with a massive trunk. The frosted vegetation diminished, and bits of green foliage and brown parts of the path appeared. After they had gone a short distance and arrived at a crossroads, Smiley said, "Look!"

Shelpa looked. He saw a sign that read SANDY BEACH. The arrow pointed to a trail on their right.

Ten minutes later, Shelpa felt sand under his feet and heard the sound of waves crashing on the shore. He also heard frantic voices. He parted several leaves the size of

elephants' ears, and after passing through a wall of vegetation, he and Smiley came out onto Sandy Beach. What
Shelpa saw reminded him of the circus in the strawberry
ice-cream scoop. Birds were flitting back and forth in
the air. Papers were strewn all over the sand. Spoons and
forks were hustling up and down the beach, hopping as
fast as their handles would go. From the top of a table on
Big Toe Hotel's patio, the knife was shouting to a crowd
of guests. "Sorry, I can't answer that. We've had no further updates. You know everything I know."

Shelpa saw the giant gargoyle in the crowd. It was
weeping, its arms around the red dragon's waist. Smoke
swirled from the dragon's nostrils as its lips blubbered
above the gargoyle's head. The dragon was sobbing, too,
drenching the gargoyle with fishbowl-sized tears.

The knife continued, "But we do have good news
about our survival guide. He was found stapled to a tree,
and the first rescue squad is working to free him."

Shelpa heard cries of "Thank goodness!" and "Oh,
that's a relief!"

"There's also some bad news, though." The knife
scratched its blade. "A tack has ambushed the second
rescue squad, and they're fighting for their lives right
now. We'll keep you posted as soon as we hear anything
new."

Sniveling, the gargoyle spoke in a hoarse, nasal voice.

"What'll happen to the boy and his flower friend when it's dark?"

"Unfortunately, the search will have to be suspended. Getting around in the forest at night is very dangerous."

"Why?" the dragon asked, speaking in a high-pitched tone. "What happens at night?"

The knife fell silent and glanced down at a place in the crowd where Shelpa could see his father standing with his arm around Shelpa's mother. Her face was buried in his shirt. Smiley's parents were by their side, huddled together and looking limp and fragile.

Shelpa cupped his hands around his mouth and yelled, "Hey! We're here! We're all right!"

The crowd reacted as if someone had screamed, "Fire!" Every head whipped around, and Shelpa could see palms pressing cheeks, hands covering mouths, and faces staring slack-jawed with eyes wide open. The knife fainted, toppled off the table, and clanged to the ground.

Mr. McStorm was the first to move, and moments later, he was crushing Shelpa to his chest. Mrs. McStorm was right behind. She hugged Shelpa with all her might, and for a second Shelpa thought he was going to choke to death. Meanwhile, Smiley's parents had their leaves wrapped around Smiley and were smothering her with kisses.

The dragon also rushed over, ditching the gargoyle. Embracing Shelpa and Smiley in its giant paws, it lifted them in the air and promptly sprayed them with slobber.

Questions flooded from their parents' mouths. "Where were you? What happened? Are you okay?"

Not knowing which question to answer first, Shelpa and Smiley were speechless, their eyes gleaming.

Shelpa looked up and saw red, orange, blue, and silver flames surrounding the Xyzyx like a lion's mane. Bright-eyed, with a beaming smile, its face was radiant and sparkling.

Mr. McStorm chuckled. He clapped a hand to his son's shoulder and said, "Never mind. You can tell us everything later. For now, just let us look at you."

CHAPTER 40

AN HOUR LATER, the sky had darkened. Campfires lit the beach and created a cozy, festive atmosphere. The smell of wood smoke and vegetable kebabs filled the air. Shelpa heard a can crack open nearby, followed by the fizzling sound of soda pouring into a glass. He turned and saw the dragon and gargoyle clink their drinks.

Smiley was sitting on her mother's lap, her eyes glued to the stick her father was holding over the fire. He was roasting a marshmallow. Shelpa sat between his parents. His mother was hunched over a knapsack, digging around for something inside. His father leaned over and put an arm around Shelpa's neck. "Listen, son. From now on, things are going to be different. I promise. I'm very proud of you."

Mr. Ray pulled the stick out of the fire pit. The marshmallow had caught fire, and he held the burning treat near his mouth and blew out the flames. He plucked the toasted marshmallow off the stick's tip and held it up. "The first marshmallow goes to you, Shelpa. Thanks for looking out for our daughter. You're an extraordinary boy. In fact, I'd say you're an extraordinary young man."

Shelpa accepted the marshmallow, but then he looked at Smiley. "To tell you the truth, this marshmallow belongs to Smiley. Without her, we'd never have made it. She deserves all the credit." He handed the marshmallow to Smiley, and she stared with wide eyes before grabbing the prize and popping it into her mouth.

Mr. McStorm pulled Shelpa closer to his side as Smiley spoke through a mouthful of marshmallow. "Shelpa, from now on, you're going to surf *every* wave to the tip of tomorrow. I just know it."

At that moment, a strange, sparkling light attracted everyone's attention. The last rays of the Xyzyx stretched like arms in the sky, spreading across the beach in a prism of light. The sun side of the Xyzyx was falling asleep as the moon side blinked. A purplish glow outlined the clouds, lingered, and then dissolved into a black, star-smothered sky, bringing the day to an end. The Xyzyx's last flash flickered on the sea, and the moon's eye opened.

Illuminated in an aura of peaceful satisfaction, Shelpa looked at Smiley and sighed. Who would have thought his new best friend would be a flower?

ABOUT THE AUTHOR

S C O T T S U S S M A N was born in Fountain Valley, California, in 1971 and currently divides his time between California and Italy. He has written many children's picture books, including *Silly the Seed, Weird the Beard, Lerky the Handturkey,* the Mark and the Molecule Maker trilogy, and *Fred and the Monster,* which won the 2015 Independent Publisher Silver Medal Award. He is currently working on his second middle-grade chapter book, which is scheduled for publication in October 2018. When not reading or writing, Scott enjoys playing the harmonica and traveling with his wife.

Contact Scott through his publisher website at
www.octopusinkpress.com

More books by

SCOTT SUSSMAN

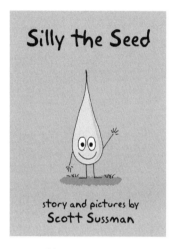

Silly the Seed

Silly the Seed is the heroic adventure of a small seed that grows up to be a beautiful flower. Along the way his acts of friendship and kindness teach and entertain readers of all ages. But when Silly needs help, who will help him?

Children's picture book, hardcover, 48 pages

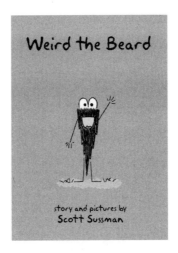

Weird the Beard

Weird the Beard is the amusing journey of a beard that makes friends by cracking jokes. But the joke's on Weird when he tries to befriend a suspicious-looking razor. Needless to say, he will never be the same.

Children's picture book, hardcover, 48 pages

Lerky the Handturkey

Lerky the Handturkey is the inspiring story of a handturkey whose wise words encourage others to see the bright side. The delightful companion to Silly the Seed and Weird the Beard, this wacky tale of friendship and optimism is a treat for every child.

Children's picture book, hardcover, 48 pages

Mark and the Molecule Maker

When Mark enters his father's laboratory and finds the Molecule Maker, he flips the switch and makes a monster. Things go from bad to worse when the creature escapes and Mark races against the sunrise to right the wrong.

Children's picture book, hardcover, 48 pages

Mark and the Molecule Maker 2:
The Lightning Jungle

The adventure continues with book two of the Mark and the Molecule Maker trilogy. When the Molecule Maker malfunctions, creating a bunch of mischievous creatures that kidnap Mark's father, Mark charges into the lightning jungle on an amazing rescue mission. But will he arrive before it's too late?

Children's picture book, hardcover, 48 pages

Mark and the Molecule Maker 3:
The Underground Mountain

In the thrilling conclusion to the Mark and the Molecule Maker trilogy, the chase is on when a cunning monster steals the Molecule Maker. In a desperate attempt to retrieve the extraordinary invention, Mark and his father must risk their lives on the treacherous underground mountain, where danger lurks behind every boulder and hides inside every hole.

Children's picture book, hardcover, 48 pages

Fred and the Monster

*National Silver Medal Winner of the
2015 Independent Publisher Awards*

Fred is afraid of the dark. So is the monster under his
bed. One night, Fred's mom does the unthinkable...
she turns off the light! Stricken with terror, Fred and
the monster must rely on each other for the courage to
confront their worst fear.

Children's picture book, hardcover, 48 pages